SWF, witty, attractive, 31 YO [actually 34],
seeks a real life in NYC. All men encouraged
to apply. Expect roadblocks.

Advance praise for *Suzanne Davis Gets a Life*

"*Suzanne Davis Gets a Life* isn't just seriously entertaining, it's entertainingly serious. Thirty-four-year-old Suzanne turns a cool eye and a sharp tongue on her Manhattan neighbors, whether they're making book club chatter or negotiating mother-child playground protocol. She looks for desirable and eligible men, but along the way finds herself facing a serious illness. I want my romantic comedy heroines to have wit, but I want them to have character too, and be as interested in the world as in themselves. Paula Marantz Cohen has given me all of that." —Margo Jefferson

A "witty commentary on contemporary life, enriched by a funny, flawed, and likable heroine." —*Kirkus*

Praise for *Jane Austen in Boca*

"Utterly charming." —*Vanity Fair*

"Page turner of the week." —*People Magazine*

Praise for *Much Ado about Jesse Kaplan*

"A brightly comic book." —*Times Literary Supplement*

"Kept me laughing from beginning to end . . . a comic tour-de-force." —*The Hudson Review*

SUZANNE DAVIS GETS A LIFE

SUZANNE DAVIS

GETS A Life

PAULA MARANTZ COHEN

PAUL DRY BOOKS
Philadelphia 2014

First Paul Dry Books Edition, 2014

Paul Dry Books, Inc.
Philadelphia, Pennsylvania
www.pauldrybooks.com

Printed in the United States of America

Library of Congress Cataloging-in-Publication Data

Cohen, Paula Marantz, 1953–
  Suzanne Davis gets a life / Paula Marantz Cohen. — First Paul Dry
Books edition.
     pages ; cm
  ISBN 978-1-58988-095-5 (alk. paper)
  1. Single women—New York (State)—New York—Fiction. 2. Self-
realization in women—Fiction. 3. Book clubs (Discussion groups)—
Fiction. I. Title.
  PS3603.O372S89 2014
  813'.54—dc23

                                        2014002968

SUZANNE DAVIS GETS A LIFE

CHAPTER

1

HERE'S SOME BACKGROUND on me: I'm thirty-one years old, single, and live in an apartment the size of a shoebox on West 76th Street in New York City.

OK—I know what you're thinking. An apartment on West 76th Street, even one the size of a shoebox, is nothing to complain about. There are people with apartments the size of shoeboxes way downtown and way uptown, not to mention in not-very-nice sections of Brooklyn, the Bronx, and New Jersey, which should make me feel grateful that my shoebox-sized apartment is much better located. That kind of comparative thinking is how people in New York in very small apartments are supposed to make themselves feel better about where they live. The only problem with comparative thinking is that it's a double-edged sword. No sooner do you start thinking about all those people in minuscule apartments in the boroughs and New Jersey than you also start thinking about all those other people in prewar sevens and humongous lofts right here in Manhattan—and before you know it, you're right back in your well-located apartment the size of a shoebox being miserable again.

You may be curious to know how I got my apartment. I bought it with the legacy from my father's death. This is also a very New York thing, where someone's loss is always someone else's gain. I can't tell you how often I've met people who told me about the death of a relative, only to say, "Upside is that I got his apartment!" The problem with the upside in my case is that I loved my dad. He gave me hope that men were not all jerks and that I might someday find one who would appreciate me. "Suzanne," he would say, "you're an exceptional young woman, and any guy who doesn't see that isn't worth the time of day." This may not sound like much, but trust me, it was the way he said it. Then he up and died of colon cancer at the age of sixty, which not only deprived me of someone I was really attached to, but also removed the buffer between me and my extremely annoying mother. So, to make a long story short, every time I turn the double locks on the metal-reinforced door of my well-located apartment the size of a shoebox, I miss my dad.

Here I need to stop and correct something I said in the heat of the moment. I'm not thirty-one years old; I'm thirty-four. Dr. Chitturi, my therapist, says lying about my age is a way of not coming to terms with who I am, and since I'm paying Dr. Chitturi $200 an hour to help me come to terms with who I am, the least I can do is take her advice and tell the truth. So—thirty-four, not thirty-one. Thirty-five in five months, if you want morbid truth-telling.

The reason I lie about my age is because if I say I'm thirty-four, people think that my biological clock must be on my mind. This bothers me for the simple reason that it is true. I think about my biological clock, like, all the time. I think things like, "If I meet some guy tomorrow, and we get married in a month, and then we started trying right away, and I get pregnant right away, I could have a baby by (fill in the date)." This is the sort of thinking that can keep you awake at two in the morning, causing you to sleep most of the next day and thereby put off, by another twenty-four-hour cycle, the chance of meeting the person you will marry in a month, etc. etc. Not that Dr. Chitturi and I aren't working on this sort of thinking; believe me, we are. But breaking toxic patterns of thought is hard, not to mention expensive (i.e., $200 an hour).

When I'm not sleeping through my biological clock, I am, despite what my mother thinks, trying to find Mr. Right. For example, I've tried Internet dating, and gone on many dates with people on JDate who went to the same summer camp as I did, and with other people on Match.com. The result hasn't been successful, though I admit that maybe it's my fault. I can only take so much reminiscing about Camp Roscowan (Native Americanese for its founder, Roz Cohen). As I see it, Internet dating is like going to the gym: you have to put in the hours on the machines if you want to get flat abs, and you have to slog through lots of bad dates to find your soul mate. I know this, but I just don't have the stamina for either one.

Moving on to what I do for a living: I'm a technical writer. I found my way to this not-very-lucrative field because I couldn't find a job when I graduated from college with a degree in English (which cost, rounding off, $120,000) and was told that there would be lots of jobs if I supplemented that degree with a one-year program in technical writing (which cost a paltry $20,000). This happens to be true. There are lots of writing jobs related to technical things like electrical circuitry and dry wall plastering. I'm not sure dry-wall plastering is technical, but it probably could pass because it's boring. Technical writing jobs are boring—they sound boring, and they are.

The particular outfit I work for is called the International Association of Air Conditioning Engineers, which pretty much sums up what they are, with the exception of the international part. As far as I can see, this is a euphemism for lots of air-conditioning engineers, most of them from New Jersey. As for the work itself, mostly what I do is write press releases on the latest air-conditioning regulations and on hot news about indoor air quality, trying to make these things interesting to the general public. To give you an example: the other day I wrote a press release with the headline "Air in 75% of Homes Is Silent Killer"—which I thought might snag the attention of your everyday non-air-conditioning-engineer type. Unfortunately, the air-conditioning engineers ended up changing my headline to: "Air in 75% of Homes May Be Unacceptable." What can I tell you? This is a cautious group of guys; they get excited about indoor air quality, even when it's not killing anyone.

Which brings me to the seemingly hopeful fact that there are primarily if not entirely guys in I-ACE. One of the small thrills of my job is being able to throw around that self-congratulatory acronym (though I have yet to actually ace anything since my fourth-grade spelling bee). But given that there are all these guys in I-ACE, you'd think that the job would be a dating bonanza. This, however, is not true. The reason? The quality of air-conditioning engineers, like the quality of air in the average home, is not very good.

Let me assure you, if you're starting to worry, that I've had my share of relationships. For example, there was a guy named Bob I met in college and lived with for three years after graduation. I did not, I admit, treat Bob well; I was biding my time until someone better came along—with the result that one day he ran off with the super-friendly girl down the hall, and they are now married and live in Montclair, New Jersey, with two kids and a dog. I can't say that I regret letting Bob get away—though from my current vantage point, his split-level house, Ford minivan, and steady job as a human resources manager make him look like he might have been more promising than I thought when he sat around the apartment playing Super Nintendo and eating jelly donuts.

I also had a relationship of slightly lesser duration with a musician named Roberto (a name with no connection whatever to his origin in a Jewish family from Larchmont, New York). Roberto played so-called "gigs" in the Village and lived hand-to-mouth. Again, this was not a great passion, and we broke up at my instigation, since it was becoming clear to me that my not-very-lucrative job with the air-conditioning engineers was pretty much supporting us both. He later went on to law school and is now making seven figures at a Manhattan law firm and married to a girl he met at Starbucks. I seem not to have understood the long-term potential of Bob and Roberto and simply judged them based on their appearance as gig-playing, jelly-donut-consuming deadbeats. Others more perceptive than I went on to reap the benefits.

I should point out that my dad (who was my biggest fan, so take this with a grain of salt) didn't like either of these guys. He said they weren't worthy of me and that, correcting for the fact that Roberto went through a Hispanic phase in high school, they both had the same first name. I hadn't even noticed this until my dad pointed it out—which says something about the attention I was paying to these relationships.

Bob and Roberto aside, I do have male friends who I can call up when I need a date for an I-ACE function or am feeling really desperate. These guys are like certain clothes that I keep in my closet under the assumption that maybe, someday, I'll wear them, even though I never do. Each time

I think about having a relationship with one of these guys, I end up deciding "not this time," and back in the closet they go.

I have other friends too, who like to hang out with me, at least on an irregular basis. These are people who laugh at my jokes—pretty much what friends are for in Manhattan. I mean if you don't have friends who laugh at your jokes, you stop trying to be funny and end up spending every night, not just two or three nights a week, eating a Lean Cuisine, watching *Entertainment Tonight* and *House Hunters*, and running out for a double scoop of gelato that you regret right after you eat it.

Of all my friends, Eleanor is the best. I've known her since the fourth grade, which means she knows my mother and so has a good grasp on why I am the way I am. If she gets really annoyed with me, I can remind her from whence I came, and she generally acknowledges my point. She's such a good friend that she doesn't even have to laugh at my jokes; she can say, "Suzanne, that's not funny"—which only a really good friend can tell you when you're being funny in a bitter, self-destructive way.

Eleanor is a free-lance art director for some of the big-name fashion magazines, which means she's around supermodels a lot and in a position to critique conventional ideas of beauty and success. Whenever I start to complain about how I look or how boring my job is, Eleanor tells me how this or that supermodel in the magazine I'm looking at is actually an anorexic, drug-addicted illiterate who has to spend hours each day striking a jaunty pose in four-inch heels. This makes me feel better for about ten minutes until the effect wears off and I go back to wishing I were a supermodel. As you can see, this is comparative thinking again: if it's not a double-edged sword, it's as long-lasting as a double scoop of gelato.

I HOPE BY NOW I've given you some idea of what my life is like. There are people in it and things happening now and then, but not much. And this, quite frankly, is the problem. I could spend the next fifty years, if I don't watch out, writing press releases for the air-conditioning engineers about unsatisfactory but not deadly indoor air quality, talking on the phone with Eleanor about why I'm lucky not to be a supermodel, re-inspecting and rejecting my collection of loser male friends, and paying (upwards of) $200 an hour to Dr. Chitturi to help me figure out who I am. Then I'd die, and that would be the end of me.

And let's face it, I want more. I'm not asking for a Jane Austen novel, but I want love or at least companionship and maybe a bigger apartment. In short, I want a life. So I've come up with this idea—"my project," as Eleanor puts it, since she and I used to do those diorama projects together in fifth grade and she thinks this is like that, only without the Elmer's Glue.

The idea came to me a few days ago when I was reading an article about speed dating. It was a newspaper clipping my mother sent me—my mother being possibly the last individual on the planet who, instead of e-mailing a link, sends newspaper articles through the mail. These articles are usually on topics like how to find romance in museum gift shops. In this case, the topic was speed dating and she'd written "Try this!" with her Sharpie in the margin.

I had actually been thinking about speed dating—Eleanor's cousin met her third husband that way—though when my mother sent me the clipping, I immediately rejected the idea. I wasn't simply being oppositional, as Dr. Chitturi would say; I was experiencing one of those revelations that sometimes need a push to become clear. The revelation I had was this: I didn't want to do speed dating; I'm not a speed-dating kind of person. The very idea of meeting so many people in such a short time made me want to crawl under the covers and meet no one for, like, forever.

And with that revelation, I also realized this: New York is big, and I'm not good at big. I don't like too many choices. I don't like ordering from menus in Greek diners or buying stockings in department stores. Two choices are fine— between string beans and broccoli or sheer and opaque, but if you throw in Brussels sprouts, summer squash, creamed asparagus, and coleslaw, I'm going to get confused; same with extra sheer and extra support and all that stuff with reinforced toes. Anyway, I was thinking about this when it came to me: Stop thinking big and start thinking small. Narrow your sights; pare down your world. Here is one area, I told myself, where Jane Austen—despite being extremely damaging to my psyche in giving me unrealistic expectations that men like Mr. Darcy actually existed—got it right. She kept things small; I would do the same. Instead of "three or four families in a country village," I'd go with a dozen or so New Yorkers in an apartment building on West 76th Street—my building, to be exact.

So that's what I would do: dig for meaning, direction, and a soul mate in my own backyard. I'd get a life without leaving home.

CHAPTER

2

As my first phase of research I decided to observe the playground behind my building.

You may be wondering why I chose to begin here, surrounded by mothers and children, when my unstated goal was to find Mr. Right or, if you prefer, Mr. Good Enough, who could be the sperm donor for the child I wanted to have before my biological clock clicked past its appointed hour. The fact is, I wanted to know the inside scoop: What had these women done to land here; how were they faring; would I fit in?

I launched my project on a Monday morning. Early—to prove to myself that I was serious. Until now, I'd gotten into the habit of sleeping late, given the laissez-faire attitude of the air-conditioning engineers regarding my work hours. But now that I had set my sights on getting a life, a change seemed called for.

My new schedule was to wake up at 7 a.m., shower, dress, and put on makeup. I didn't need to wear makeup to go to a playground, but I'd been conditioned to put it on because I could hear my mother's voice in my head saying, "You never know who you're going to meet. Don't you want to put on a little lipstick?" I was therefore nicely made up and able to arrive at the playground behind my building at around 7:45. Once there, I positioned myself on a bench with a good view of the proceedings.

The mothers with the hyperactive children began to arrive around 8 A.M., with most of the regulars making an appearance by 9. This put me in place to watch the entire spectacle of mother-child interaction until the group's late-morning retreat for lunch and nap.

I should note here that all in attendance at the playground were the actual mothers of the children in question, itself a novelty when you consider that this is Manhattan, where it is standard practice to shunt the labor-intensive aspects of child rearing onto a nanny while keeping the good stuff, like making cupcakes and reading Dr. Seuss books, for yourself. But given that my address was not among the swankier ones on the Upper West Side, and given that such staples as prepared food and Starbucks lattes can dig into even a substantial income, many of the mothers in my building were shouldering the child-care burden themselves (with occasional help from foreign exchange students and accommodating, if annoying, mothers-in-law). As for the handful of nannies who *were* associated with the building, they had chosen to congregate elsewhere, which, I have to say, I could understand. It's one thing to see a child as your job, another thing entirely to see said child as an extension of yourself—and the crazed intensity of the latter persuasion might reasonably cause those of the former to want to keep their distance. As a result of this fact, my building's playground presented what one might call a "pure sample of biological motherhood."

My vigil soon yielded some superficial observations. For example, all the mothers carried flowered Vera Bradley quilted duffel bags that contained the following staples: a half-dozen assorted juice boxes, a Ziploc bag of Cheerios, a jumbo container of disposable wipes, a small, picturesquely tattered blanket, and a few extra pairs of underpants.

Despite the sameness of these items, the mothers themselves varied in certain predictable ways. I soon identified three distinct groups. First were the dazed looking very young mothers, who seemed to be wondering how it was that they had gotten here. When had they gone in a blink of an eye from the college classroom, where they had whiled away their time tracing the names of their boyfriends in their notebooks, to being saddled with kids who were whining and pulling at them every minute of every day? You could see how befuddled they were by it all. If they were comic strip characters, they would have had thought balloons with question marks in them emerging from their heads.

The second group of mothers were slightly older and therefore less befuddled. They had spent enough time in the workplace to realize how deadly dull it was and to be mildly exultant (if a little guilty, given those feminist texts about self-actualization they'd read in college) to be released into the world of PB&J sandwiches and time-outs. OK, it wasn't always scintillating, but it was way better than working for that bitch in marketing who had kept making them re-do their spreadsheets.

Finally, there was the smattering of really old mothers, who had just managed to beat their biological clocks and for whom motherhood represented a deeply desired shift in the nature of their universe. The smallest details of child care fascinated these women; they couldn't get enough of them, which made you worry about the recipients of their attention. All that care—how could it not result in serious neurosis?

Seated off to the side of the play area, I was in a position to survey this scene. I have to admit that I liked watching the kids at play. It's not that I like kids exactly—that would be going too far—but I don't dislike them, which is what distinguishes me from my friend Eleanor. She freely acknowledges that, for her, children fall into one of two categories: extremely annoying and outright loathsome. Cute just doesn't come into it at all for her. Eleanor's biological clock seems to be broken: "No children for me, thank you," she likes to say, "I've already had my share." She is referring to Ronnie, her ex-husband, recently indicted for insider trading, who, I admit, is as close to an infant as a grown man can get. Still, in fairness to Ronnie, Eleanor never had any maternal instincts, as far as I could see, and I've known her since the fourth grade. Even when I point out a toddler in the supermarket in one of those outfits—if it's a boy, there's usually a vest involved, and if it's a girl, a headband with a floppy flower—and say, "Isn't that adorable?," Eleanor always says, "No. He/she looks like a dressed-up monkey." And when the kid throws a tantrum on the checkout line, holding everyone up as the mom tries valiantly to reason with what is clearly an irrational creature, she says, "Don't tell me you think that's cute, too." And the truth is that though I don't, exactly, I know I probably would if the child were mine. This, I surmise, is what qualifies me to be a mother.

But getting back to my morning vigil. You might think that the mothers in the play area would be disturbed seeing me there, sitting for hours watching their children play. But this turns out not to be the case. While a man lingering in the vicinity of a playground would immediately be assumed to be a pedophile, a woman, unless she has excessive tattooing or unseemly cleavage, is felt to be vicariously indulging her maternal instincts. This is a double standard that, if I were a man, I might consider protesting, but as a woman I am content to leave alone.

So there I was, sitting on my bench, surveying the playground scene for a few days. I should note that the more I watched, the more I saw a definite pattern to the proceedings. It went like this: The kids would be playing, and the mothers would be talking for a while among themselves. Then, one of the mothers would suddenly turn her head and bark at the kid she had all the time been watching out of the corner of her eye (though seemingly deep in conversation about biodegradable wipes): "Caitlin, take that out of your mouth. Did you hear me?" Or: "Jacob, stop hitting Spencer. Jacob—what-did-I say! I want you over here this minute!"

When these commands were barked out, the other mothers would halt their conversation and watch for the results. Did Caitlin take whatever it was out of her mouth? Did Jacob stop hitting Spencer? If the order was followed, talk would resume smoothly; if not, the other mothers would sigh in mock sympathy and give the mother in question an invisible demerit, after which things would proceed, until another mother (or sometimes the same one) would feel obliged to bark out another order that would be effectively followed or ignored—and so on.

I'd been sitting on the bench for three days surveying this ebb and flow before I made what an anthropologist would call "contact." It was during the early part of the morning, when only one mother and child had made an appearance. Having eavesdropped on the playground mothers over the past few days, I knew that the mother in question was named Iris. I now had occasion to speak with her, when her child, a four-year-old boy with a small scrunched-up face, began hurling dirt near where I was pretending to read *The New Yorker*. Iris came over and apologized, and I said it was no problem; her kid was free to dig near me if he wanted; I enjoyed watching him; he was adorable. Saying a child is adorable is de rigueur if you want to have any standing with the mother. Iris seemed pleased when I said it. In point of fact, he looked like a ferret—a ferret with a certain wild charm, it's true, but I guessed he was rarely described as adorable, except by his grandparents.

The day after my initial contact with Iris, I decided to build on the headway I'd made by bringing her child a small snack. I thought a lot about what to bring, knowing how important food is in the maternal lexicon, and, after contemplating a number of possibilities, settled on a mandarin orange. A mandarin orange struck me as just the right choice. For one thing, it's not threatening—you can't poison a mandarin orange very easily. For another, it's a bit out of the ordinary: not a banana or a regular orange, which would seem to lack imagination. Finally, of course, it's healthy, and one thing these Upper West Side mothers are into is health. In a few years, they'll be grateful if their kids aren't snorting cocaine, but for now, they're serious about soy products and avoiding refined sugar.

As I had hypothesized, the mandarin orange went over well. It seemed that Iris had forgotten to bring snack that day (not "a snack" but "snack," in the parlance of the playground; the dropping of articles is one of those tics that seems to set in when women start taking their mothering lifestyle seriously). She said oranges were a special favorite of Daniel's, though she didn't know that he'd ever had a mandarin orange.

"Have you ever had a mandarin orange, Daniel?" she asked. "This nice lady is offering you one."

Daniel looked at me with suspicion.

"You can take it," said his mother, "but say thank you."

I could see that Daniel was in a tug of war with himself. Part of him didn't want to take the orange. It was in his nature to be suspicious, both because it had been drummed into him to beware of strangers (and he was not yet clear about when a person ceased to be one) and because he sensed that I had ulterior motives. Though he wasn't sure what he was being bribed for, he could tell that manipulation of some sort was in the air. But the orange looked nice; it was bright and smooth, so he took it.

"Shall I peel it for you?" I asked.

Daniel, however, was now through with me. He gave the orange to his mother to peel and turned his face away in what mothers call shyness but which I know really amounts to plain old dislike.

"I told you to say 'thank you,'" said Iris, irritated not only at Daniel but also at me for having provoked a situation where her mothering skills were being tested and found wanting.

"It's OK," I said. "I read somewhere that kids shouldn't have to say 'thank you' when they're this age. If they come to it on their own when they're older, it's more genuine." I had not, in fact, read this; I had extrapolated it from my own experience, since my mother had forced me to say "please" and "thank you" in every possible transaction, and I had grown up with a profound distrust for these terms. In short, I was on Daniel's side here—another example of what Eleanor has termed my natural mothering instincts. Iris, who had difficulty getting Daniel to do anything, looked relieved.

"Are you a writer?" she asked, after the orange had been peeled, sampled, and discarded, and Daniel had run off to shove one of the smaller toddlers around. I wondered where she had gotten this idea and realized that I had, during my vigil, sometimes jotted things down on a pad in my pocket, mostly grocery lists or random points to be added to I-ACE press releases.

"I suppose I am," I said carefully. I had occasionally thought about writing something—who hasn't?—so why not make it official, since this would give my presence at the playground an elevated creative purpose that Iris could respect.

"That's so neat," she said. "I used to write poetry in college."

"I could never write poetry," I said, which is true and, again, just the right thing to say. It united Iris and me as fellow writers with no future who were not in competition with each other.

"Actually, I make my living doing technical writing," I continued. "Only I work mostly at home, and I like to think about more creative things in the morning. Watching the children play is very inspiring."

Iris nodded. She seemed to find it altogether natural that, without a child of my own, I would be inspired in the presence of Daniel.

Other mothers had by now begun to appear on the playground, their children in tow. I had already taken particular stock of two of these women, regulars who seemed to represent two extremes among the older mothers. One was a woman in her mid-forties named Karen, who, based on my eavesdropping, I knew to be the haggard veteran of many infertility treatments. She was among the most nervous of the mothers, her eyes continually darting toward the fragile specimen of a child in padded clothing whom she had incubated. Karen, I had gleaned, was once a financial analyst, her dry demeanor and no-nonsense air suggesting that she was more at home dealing with large abstract sums of money than the mood swings of a four year old. Her husband, also in finance, periodically made an appearance on the playground to confer about some detail relating to their child: the effectiveness of the special ointment on the rash behind the right ear, the consistency of the last bowel movement, the girding of the loins for the next vaccine. He and Karen had a look of barely suppressed hysteria as they confronted the prospect of overseeing the life of another human being who was worth, given the outlay required for his conception and ongoing hothouse care, more than the GNP of a small African nation.

The other older mother was named Pauline. Whereas Karen was rather nondescript and WASP-y, wore Talbots blouses, and was soft-spoken if tightly wound, Pauline had a dramatically Semitic profile, wore black leggings and turtle-neck sweaters, and spoke with a snappish authority that made even the most recalcitrant preschooler jump to attention. I had heard her reprimand Daniel (Iris's child), who had elbowed the delicate Matthew (Karen's progeny), with a sharpness that had brought Daniel practically to his knees. Pauline's own child, Rose, was a soulful, deliberate creature who often stood scrutinizing the swing as if trying to decide whether it was worthwhile to give it a try, invariably concluding that it wasn't. Pauline was a former intellectual property lawyer married to a mayoral aide, and she could often be heard pontificating to a group of cowed other mothers about what, "under no circumstances," she would permit her child to do. The forbidden activities included eating candy (Rose had been tricked into thinking pineapple was candy), watching television (only DVDs recommended by a professor at Columbia Teachers College), and playing in a sandbox (thanks to an episode of *House* where a child contracted a virulent and—were it not for House's diagnostic skills—deadly MRSA).

Now that Daniel was occupied with the other children, Iris was free to take advantage of being left unencumbered for a rare interval, and called out to the other women that they should come over to meet me. This fell largely on deaf ears for the reason that there was a brouhaha in progress regarding the mid-morning distribution of the juice boxes, an event that occurs ritualistically at 10 A.M. Today, one box appeared to be missing its affixed plastic straw, giving rise to high-level deliberations as to how the juice in the defective box was going to be accessed. The mothers were bent over the box and did not raise their heads to respond to Iris's call—with the exception of Pauline. I knew Pauline had had me in her sights since I'd begun sitting on the bench, and had probably hoped that she would be the first to delve into my back story. But even though Iris had beaten her to it, she was still interested, so she extricated herself from the juice-box controversy and came over.

"I want you to meet someone new," Iris said to Pauline. "This is . . . ?" She cued me to fill in the blank.

"Suzanne Davis," I said.

"Suzanne," repeated Iris to Pauline. "Suzanne is a writer." I had noticed that the playground mothers applied the same simple speech patterns used with their young children to all conversations, having apparently forgotten that in the adult world pronouns and subordinate clauses were often used.

"Pauline Gartenberg," said Pauline, looking at me approvingly. A writer is always welcome on the Upper West Side of Manhattan.

I quickly explained about the air-conditioning engineers, which did not seem to faze her. It was understood that being a writer didn't necessarily mean you were a successful one— indeed, it was better if you weren't successful since it left everyone free to believe in your talent without having to be jealous of you.

"Which one is yours?" I asked, casting my eyes around queryingly. Of course, I knew which one was hers, but the ritual of the playground involved paying deference to the child, in the manner of fealty to a sovereign. Once that was done, one could move on to other things.

"That's Rose." She pointed to the sallow-faced moppet with doleful eyes who was studying the slide before deciding not to slide down it.

"What an intelligent face," I remarked.

Pauline nodded. "Everyone thinks I'm her grandmother."

I waved a hand to suggest this was ridiculous, but I have to admit that Pauline looked pretty old. I had noted this the first day, and had indeed thought she was the child's grandmother until I saw the dexterous way she unzipped the flannel duffel bag and the surety with which she put the straw in the juice box. The sight of the elderly Pauline had, truth be told, lifted my spirits considerably. Vistas of extra time seemed to unfold by her example. "How old were you when you had her?" I asked, trying to sound nonchalant.

"Forty-five. Five years older than Karen." She motioned to the nervous mother hovering near the child on the swing set. "Roger and I hadn't intended to have children and then one day I said, 'Why not?' and wham!—I was pregnant a month later."

Both Iris and I listened to this with admiration. Considering what Karen had gone through in order to conceive, Pauline's story had a quality of the miraculous about it. Then again, one wondered if Karen had just been trying too hard or hadn't put the right spirit into it (the "wham" of Pauline's account suggested a zest that Karen might not be capable of).

"I'm the poster child for plenty of time," noted Pauline—then paused to appraise me more closely. "Do you have one?"

she finally asked. The form of this question, at once casual and focused, suggested that having a child was akin to having a desirable if slightly out-of-date commodity, like one of those Tiffany bracelets with the dangling heart that everyone had a few years ago.

"No," I said, feeling it best to be direct. "I don't even have a husband."

Pauline cocked her head, as if listening to the ticking of my biological clock. I tried to look unperturbed, but I could tell that she was onto me. Even if I'd told her I was thirty-one, she would have sniffed out the missing three and a half years in a heartbeat.

"You should come to my book club," she finally said. "We're doing all the books we were assigned in college but didn't bother to read. Next week it's *The Great Gatsby*. As a writer, I'm sure you'd add a lot to our discussion."

I told her I didn't know about that, but Pauline wasn't listening. She had made up her mind about me and nothing I could say would make a difference. It was a style familiar to me from my mother, and I felt a pang for little Rose and the years of therapy that lay ahead as a result of so much benign intervention.

"Tuesday, 8 P.M., Apartment 5J." She scribbled this information on a work sheet that she extracted from her Vera Bradley flannel satchel, then added with a certain briskness: "There's someone in the group who I think might be right for you. I can't promise, but my instincts are usually good."

Of course, I said I'd come. I didn't mind discussing *The Great Gatsby*; I'd been an English major in college and knew it well, having read it three or four times (it happens to be one of those books taught over and over again, probably because the professors are too lazy to read new ones). It would be nice to pretend that I didn't know *The Great Gatsby* as well as I did and thus gain points for being smarter than I was. Besides, I could use some intellectual stimulation. Eleanor and I mostly talked about things like which one of us Mrs. Moynihan, our fourth-grade teacher, had liked better, and whether our junior-high-school gym suits had been forest green or pea green. Most of my friends with whom I might once have had an intelligent conversation had married and moved to the suburbs, where their mental energy was focused on organic lawn fertilizer and finishing their basements. In comparison to these people (some of whom didn't even have children yet), a woman like Pauline seemed a veritable Einstein.

Finally, I intuited that I could do worse than put myself into the capable hands of Pauline Gartenberg. Given her efficiency in procreation, she seemed just the right person to help me with my biological clock.

CHAPTER

3

THE APARTMENT OF Pauline Gartenberg, the site of the book club meeting, was a medium-sized three-bedroom decorated in the minimalist style favored by those Upper West Siders who don't go in for cluttered Victorian. One or the other of these two styles is, from my experience, the norm among the inhabitants of this part of the city. In Pauline's case, there were a few colorful throws and pillows on the furniture and large pieces of abstract art on the walls, including what looked to be a cubist portrait of Pauline over the mantel. The members of the book club were all perched on metallic and leather chairs and sofas, very low to the ground, as though they were sitting around a modernist campfire.

Pauline, who had exchanged her leggings and turtle neck for a loose, tent-like dress, was clearly in control of the pro-ceedings, while her husband, Roger, a short, bearded man in a bright geometrically patterned sweater, was pouring wine and passing out hummus and crackers.

I had arrived ten minutes late, and Pauline chastised me. "We treat book club seriously," she explained, giving me the kind of look she might have given Rose for not putting her napkin on her lap. (As with "snack," "book club" was used without the article, suggesting a mysterious kinship between the two activities.)

My face got very red at being reprimanded by Pauline, a holdover from having suffered so much criticism from my mother over the years—at least this is what my $200-an-hour therapist, Dr. Chitturi, says is the reason I'm so sensitive. Once I had taken a breath and told myself that Pauline was not my mother (what Dr. Chitturi has instructed me to remember in such circumstances), I looked around at the group, curious to see who had gathered for the purpose of discussing *The Great Gatsby*.

I recognized one couple, perched on the low chairs in front of the low coffee table, as Karen and David, the parents of the in-vitro-generated Matthew from the playground. Karen was clutching her cell phone, in case the babysitter in their apartment downstairs should call with a problem. Another couple, introduced as Marsha and Herb, were sprawled in a floppy, exhausted fashion on the sofa across from the chairs. Marsha was a juvenile court judge and Herb was a social worker. Both had the frayed look of people used to struggling all day long to be sympathetic, their bodies collapsed into a kind of permanent shrug, as if to say, "What more can I do?"

As Pauline promised, there were also single men present—two of them, judging from the absence of accompanying females—both seated on large throw cushions on the floor, so as to guarantee that they looked completely ridiculous. One was a slight man with wispy blond hair of about my age. Pauline introduced him as Stephen Danziger and explained that he lived in 4H. I had, as a matter of fact, seen him once or twice in the elevator, where he had volunteered the fact that he was a math teacher on his way to the high school where he taught in the South Bronx. We may have chatted briefly on these occasions, but, in truth, I can't recall. I took his occupation to mean that he was either an insufferable do-gooder or a pathetic loser and promptly forgot all about him. (This is the kind of dismissive thinking, by the way, that Dr. Chitturi says reflects my own deep-seated insecurities and that we're working on ridding me of at $200 an hour.)

Seated on the other cushion was a dark-haired man of about forty who, like Roger, was wearing a colorful patterned sweater. More imposing in his build than the wispy Stephen, this man had the sort of large, emphatic features that, on the Upper West Side, are viewed as handsome by women who can't afford to be too aesthetically discriminating. Pauline introduced him as Derek Newman and said that he worked with Roger in the mayor's office.

I shook everyone's hand, and Derek looked into my eyes with the mock soulfulness of the soon-to-be divorced man trying to communicate that he is open to your charms but not sure how to proceed.

Everyone was holding a copy of *The Great Gatsby*.

Pauline began the discussion by saying that critics called *The Great Gatsby* the Great American Novel. Did we agree?

"I thought *Huckleberry Finn* was the Great American Novel," said Herb, slouching lower in the sofa and shoveling another cracker with hummus into his mouth.

"*Huckleberry Finn* for the nineteenth century. *The Great Gatsby* for the twentieth," clarified Pauline.

There was some discussion about what it meant to be the Great American Novel and whether things had changed now that we were in the twenty-first century. Roger said he didn't think so, given that Fitzgerald was critiquing the materialist values of American society; that could still hold today.

"It holds but it's not a fresh idea anymore," said Derek. "We all know material success is hollow. What else is new?"

"It's all in the treatment," said Roger. "You say it's not fresh; I say it's timeless."

"I agree," said Herb. "My clients are into materialism; they're all Gatsbys" (lots of Herb's clients were drug dealers).

There was discussion about Gatsby in the ghetto and what that meant.

"I don't think it's materialism that matters so much; it's relationship—that's what drives Gatsby to *be* a materialist," noted Marsha. "It's the hopeful element in the novel. He wants to be in a relationship, even if it's an impossible one. The kids I see in court don't understand long-term commitment and responsibility. Maybe it's the generation."

"I don't think you can generalize," proffered Stephen, the wispy math teacher. Why is it that someone always has to make the bleeding-heart point that "it's impossible to generalize"? To his credit, however, Stephen proceeded: "My father used to say that kids 'nowadays'—which would have been our 'old days'—had no sense of responsibility. Now we say the same thing. I see all kinds at my school. But I imagine you"—he nodded in acknowledgment of Marsha—"see a self-selected group of incorrigibles."

"Well, they seem more incorrigible than they used to be," grumbled Marsha, "though maybe I'm just getting older."

"I'm afraid you're off point," interrupted Pauline, who appeared to keep book club, the way she kept her child, on a very short leash. "Getting back to Gatsby . . ."

"What did he want anyway?" complained Karen. As a former financial analyst, she spoke as though she was searching for Fitzgerald's bottom line and not finding it.

"What did he want?" Roger took this up. "Admiration and respect. What all men want."

"Power and money," said David. "What all men want."

"The unattainable, ideal woman," contributed Derek. "What all men want."

At this juncture, I felt I should say something. I'd been silent out of a mix of trying to project polite reserve and wanting to gauge the best tone with which to make a contribution. But you can only hold out for so long in this sort of situation. At a certain point, if you don't speak up, you look like a dud who doesn't have opinions.

"As your comments indicate, it's a very male book," I contributed, trying to sound both authoritative and obsequious—a combination that may be the only marketable skill that accompanies a degree in English. "This may be why issues of responsibility and commitment don't figure in it." This, I should note, had been the consensus about almost everything we read in my Women's Studies course in college, and I now embellished the idea accordingly: "Daisy is an object. And Gatsby never thinks about things women would consider—like having children. He doesn't take into account that Daisy is a mother. Fitzgerald doesn't either. It's a negligible aspect of the plot."

My observation was greeted favorably by Pauline and Karen, who said that now that they thought about it, the lack of attention paid to Daisy's daughter in the book bothered them. It made for a sterile, unrealistic atmosphere.

"Are you saying all books have to care about children?" asked Stephen, the wispy math teacher, with some amusement.

"Not all," I acknowledged. "We wouldn't want babies in *Moby Dick*."

"I don't know," said the wispy Stephen. "That book needed to lighten up, if I remember correctly."

"I agree," I nodded—I'd never gotten through *Moby Dick* in college. "But then, Melville would have bored us with details about cloth versus disposable diapers."

I could tell that Stephen would have liked to continue with this riff, but Pauline would have none of it. "Attention to children helps to humanize the characters," she asserted authoritatively. "If they're ignored, it says something."

"I don't know that Daisy's child is completely ignored," said Stephen. "It says here"—he riffled through the pages— "'he'—that's Gatsby—'kept looking at the child with surprise. I don't think he had ever really believed in its existence before.'"

I was momentarily impressed by the wispy Stephen's ability to call up this relevant passage.

"Do you think he thinks the child is his?" asked Roger, perking up at this possible plot line.

"Not at all," I pronounced. "There was no logistical way this could happen. Besides, it would go against the grain of Gatsby's idealism: he wanted Daisy's image unsullied."

Pauline, however, was intent on returning to the subject of the child. "Note that he refers to the little girl as an 'it,'" she pointed out. "That's telling. Gatsby is shocked to see her because it shatters his dream of being with Daisy alone. The child makes this impossible."

"That's an understatement," Roger piped up. "A kid is the end of your sex life, let me tell you."

Pauline shot him a look, and Roger passed the hummus around again. This lightened the mood. A discussion of children in literature followed, segueing into children's books and how Pauline intended to write one, if only she had the time.

Rose was brought out in a frilly nightgown to say good night, with everyone asking her questions that Pauline answered for her. After the child was trundled off to bed, Pauline seemed to feel that we had put in our time talking about the book and could now veer off onto the subject of child rearing, about which everyone, with the exception of myself and the wispy Stephen, had something to say. Derek had two children, though he was less interested in talking about them than about the bitter feelings he harbored against his spouse, whom he was currently in the process of divorcing. He brought everyone up to date: "I can't believe that she was so sweet when I married her and now she's such a bitch."

"People change," noted Roger.

"Or maybe she was always a bitch and you didn't realize it," said Herb.

Derek sighed. "I wonder how I'll ever trust a woman again." He glanced in my direction.

"That's a bad attitude to take," said Pauline.

"I'm just saying." Derek sighed again. "When you've been hurt, it's hard to be trusting. Someone can look loving and honest and turn out to be vicious and deceitful." His eyes darted in my direction again, as though to say that I, for example, might look loving and honest and not be.

"I'm not going to bad-mouth your ex," said Pauline. "I remember how much she contributed to our discussion of *To the Lighthouse*—but it didn't take a rocket scientist to see that she was a piece of work."

"You can't generalize based on one bad experience," noted Stephen, a statement in line with his earlier refusal to generalize about the kids in his high school, thereby confirming my suspicion that he *was* an insufferable do-gooder, if not also a pathetic loser (categories which are not, after all, mutually exclusive).

Derek nodded wearily. "I know what you mean. I can't lose my trust in all women just because one happened to hurt me. I know there are generous, uncomplaining, loving women out there. I just have to be open to them."

It was a daunting set of adjectives, and I have to say I lowered my eyes so as not to suggest that they had anything to do with me. It wouldn't have been right to lead him on that way.

CHAPTER

4

Still, I was not surprised when, the next evening, Derek called to ask me out.

"I immediately felt a kinship with you," he explained. "And when Pauline told me you might be available, I didn't want to waste any time. As you could probably see, I've learned a lot since my marriage—I'm a more sensitive person now. Not that I'm entirely divorced yet, but I'm on my way; you can be certain about that."

I told him I took his word for the certainty of the divorce. As for the sensitivity, I can't say that I had seen evidence of it, nor was his forlorn manner of speaking particularly romantic. But I was in no position to be picky. I had promised myself (and Dr. Chitturi) to allow ample time to evaluate people and not jump to conclusions the way I usually did. So I agreed to have dinner with Derek the next night at the Chinese restaurant a few blocks up on Broadway.

When I arrived, he was already there and had ordered a bowl of hot-and-sour soup because, he said, he was hungry and couldn't wait. He looked depressed and eager to tell me about his day.

He had just spent the afternoon with his kids. Since the separation, Derek had been thrust into the novel position of having to entertain his two children by himself for hours at a time, sometimes even for days. He found this grueling.

"I'm sure you'll get the hang of it," I reassured him.

"I don't know," he sighed. "I don't have the skills. I think it's something women are born with."

From my experience, the biological argument is one men drag out when they want to fob off on you something they don't want to do. So when Derek said this, I should have been alert to potential problems, but you know how it is: when you're starved for love and companionship, you tend to let things go that should send you running in the other direction.

We proceeded to eat our General Tso's chicken and talk about a variety of topics: *The Great Gatsby*, what it was like to work in the mayor's office, indoor air quality, and the strains of being a single father. The conversation moved along, and Derek apparently thought we had hit it off. When he took me to my door he said: "I really like you." Then, he leaned in and kissed me—a long yet perfunctory kiss. "I'd come in," he said, "but I'm exhausted."

I was a little surprised by the first part of this statement. I hadn't invited him in. But I could definitely see that he was exhausted. He was leaning against my door as if propping himself up, and I had to practically bite my lip not to tell him that I had a pullout couch he could use if he wanted. I restrained myself, however, and said, "I can see that you're very tired." This is what you're supposed to say to show your concern but not turn yourself into a doormat. I learned this from Dr. Chitturi, who is always saying: "I can see that you are very distressed," but never asking me to sleep on *her* pullout couch.

"The kids, you know," said Derek by way of explanation. "I was with them all afternoon, and they really gave me a workout."

I nodded.

"But tomorrow, I'll be refreshed."

And so he was. The next night, after dinner at the Hungarian place on Amsterdam, Derek came home with me. I had straightened up the apartment in anticipation of this prospect, stacking all the I-ACE material in one corner, draping the afghan I'd bought at a craft fair and never used over the bed, and hanging up the poster from the Cezanne exhibit that had been rolled up in the corner for six months over my pullout couch.

Derek, however, did not seem to notice any of this. He was not someone with much awareness of his surroundings. I would later learn that he lived in a squalid one bedroom downtown—his wife having kept the spacious apartment in the Village.

"I married pretty young, and my wife didn't like sex much, so you can imagine," he explained by way of prelude. And, indeed, once we had retired to my bedroom, which really involved walking a few feet to the area adjacent to the kitchen, I learned that his lovemaking technique was nothing to write home about, as my mother would say. Still, he had staying power, and we both emerged with an acceptable level of breathlessness.

I have to say that hot sex, though much hyped in certain quarters, isn't high on my list of prerequisites for a lasting relationship. I'm looking for human decency and maybe some good conversation. To expect sexual prowess on top of these things would be unrealistic.

So that's how my affair with Derek began, although the word "affair," with its suggestion of tumultuous goings-on, does not seem entirely apt. Our relationship mostly took the form of a foursome with his two impossible kids. Derek was not any more practiced as a father than as a lover, but his kids would have been a challenge for the most diligent supermom.

Brad, the eight year old, had been diagnosed with hyper-activity disorder and had a schedule for regular doses of Rita-lin, which he adamantly refused to take. Josh, the six year old, was petulant and quietly nasty, presumably owing to the fact that so much attention was being lavished on his hyper-active brother. Still, no amount of cajoling and sucking up seemed to work with Josh; his modus operandi was to stand sullenly in the corner and ignore all efforts to get him to do what was expected of him.

"Come on, Josh, let's put your jacket on and go out and play," Derek would say, hoping to get the ricocheting Brad outside to expend some of his excess energy. But Josh would dig in his heels and refuse to budge. Often, this would result in my staying inside with Josh while Derek went outside with Brad, though as soon as they left, Josh would dissolve into tears at having been abandoned.

I have to admit that I could understand Josh's behavior. He was acting out the impossibility of his situation. Sad-dled with warring parents and an older sibling with impulse-control problems, where did he fit in? What did he get out of this whole thing? I understood his stubbornness and his subsequent tantrums. I also found him to be an unmitigated pain in the ass.

Eventually I hit on the idea of feeding him candy. Manda-rin oranges just wouldn't do the trick here; what was needed was serious sugar—the sort that causes hyperglycemia and tooth decay. Plus, what can I say? I happen to like candy my-self, and hanging out with Josh allowed me to indulge my fondness for Sour Patch Kids and Reese's Peanut Butter Cups. Moreover, as I was only in the presence of this child for a few hours before he was returned to his mother, the candy solution served the double duty of making him more amenable with me and more impossible with her (given that the sugar high would wear off by the time he was handed back). It's true that his mother hadn't done anything to me directly—I hadn't even met her—but my grievance, though abstract, was genuine: this kid was hers and not mine, and what was I doing taking care of him anyway?

You'll say that my behavior was pretty reprehensible, and some of you health nuts are going to say I skirted child abuse. I admit that, sometimes, after feeding Josh from my Sour Patch stash, I'd feel this wave of guilt pass over me, thinking about how the poor child, years from now, would have rotten teeth and an addiction to refined sugar. But then it occurred to me that my mother had never thought twice about feeding me candy—I mean, there was a time, in the not so distant past, when candy wasn't equated with heroin—and I hadn't turned out so bad, had I? OK, don't answer that.

The truth is that Josh and I got along pretty well when we were pumping our jaws over the saltwater taffy that I'd bought during an ill-fated trip to the Jersey shore last summer. That was the mini-vacation I took with a guy who spent most of the time talking on my cell phone to his "aunt" in California, having conveniently left *his* phone in the motor lodge, resulting in an astronomical roving charge that he didn't pay because, subsequent to that vacation, he headed out to California to be with his "aunt" and never to return. But I am digressing. My only point is that Josh and I bonded, in a manner of speaking, over candy.

Later, I asked Derek if his ex-wife, who, after all, had primary responsibility for the kids, had anyone to help her out.

"No," he said. "Her mother comes by once a week so she can go to yoga, but other than that, she's on her own."

"That's pretty impressive," I said.

Derek, used to thinking of his wife as a harridan who was trying to soak him for all he was worth, considered this for a moment. "I suppose it is," he said and grew quiet for a while, until he realized that Brad had barricaded himself in the bathroom and was repeatedly flushing the toilet while screaming at the top of his lungs. Some high-level negotiation had to ensue between father and son through the bathroom door, so Josh and I retreated to Derek's bedroom with our Tootsie Pops to play Nintendo.

ALONG WITH HELPING him with his children, I also accompanied Derek to events related to his job in the mayor's office. We were invariably seated with the Gartenbergs, since he and Roger worked together. While Roger and Derek talked business, Pauline discoursed with me, mostly about Rose's precocious development.

One evening, however, our conversation took a different turn. It was approximately four months into my relationship with Derek, and we were seated with Pauline and Roger at the mayor's black-tie gala for the Transit Authority, about to dig into our poached salmon and julienne vegetables. Derek and Roger were deep into discussing the impending sanitation workers' strike when Pauline leaned forward in a confidential manner: "I've wanted to speak to you about something, since I know you're smitten with Derek," she said.

I had not realized that I seemed smitten with Derek. The idea that anyone could be smitten with Derek, whose modest good looks did not wear well on continued viewing, was, to my mind, unlikely. But I chalked Pauline's phrasing up to the naturally hyperbolic tendencies that women get into when they speak about men, given how few functional ones there are out there, especially in New York. Besides, there's no accounting for tastes, and Roger, Pauline's husband, was no Brad Pitt either.

"My only concern," she said now, continuing her confidential whisper, "is that he might not want to have more children."

I have to say that Pauline's remark gave me a jolt. You may think that this is a conclusion that I would have arrived at on my own: a man in his forties with a depleted bank account and two out-of-control kids might not, it could be deduced, feel a pressing need for further procreation. But for some reason, I hadn't thought of that. I had proceeded under the assumption that if you became involved with someone, then married him, you then, inevitably, had children with him, unless some physiological impediment reared its head, in which case you expended a great deal of time and money on fertility specialists and, if that failed, you adopted from China.

I had, you might say, been continuing on with Derek on automatic pilot, with this scenario in mind. I imagined, I suppose, that once I married Derek, his impossible children would be returned to that other world whence they had come and that I would then proceed to have my own impossible children, who would not seem so impossible since they would be mine. If pressed, I would have admitted that I wouldn't want to sever my relationship with Brad and Josh entirely; I would simply bestow upon them a half-brother and half-sister (my mixed-gender preference). But *not* to have children of my own? I could see how this might be fine for some people—Eleanor, for example—but for me, children were part of the marital package. They were a nonnegotiable item.

"I know you've thought about this," said Pauline, making me feel all the more blockheaded for not having thought of it. "I may be wrong, of course. And since he's crazy about you, he might want more children."

Again, the notion that Derek was crazy about me, given our rather perfunctory lovemaking, struck a false note.

"But there's also the financial factor," said Pauline. "Bathsheba plans to bleed him for every last cent."

I have neglected to mention that Derek's wife's name was Bathsheba. This in itself might have been a warning that her hold on his financial future might assume Biblical proportions.

"She wants to send the boys to Ethical Culture or Jewish Day School," continued Pauline.

This struck me as a slightly odd set of educational alternatives, but regardless, an expensive one. I must have had a shell-shocked look because Pauline now moved into damage-control mode: "I don't mean to be a naysayer," she hurried to amend, "I mean, I introduced you—though I may have thought that Stephen would be better"—I recalled that Stephen was the wispy math teacher and insufferable do-gooder/loser—"and Derek does have steady work, unless of course the recession gets so bad that the mayoral staff will have to be cut, and even Roger worries about that and he's been there five years longer. . . ." She trailed off. But she had painted a vivid picture: Derek possibly losing his job, with two unmanageable children and a harridan of a soon-to-be ex-wife who intended to bleed him dry. What was I getting myself into?

This conversation put a damper on my next evening with Derek, when we went for Indian food on lower Lexington Avenue and then up to my apartment for a night of love, which is to say, a stretch of heaving and shifting, culminating in Derek's groaning loudly and sinking back onto the pillow.

Normally this would have been succeeded by his drifting off immediately into a deep if restless slumber, but tonight he sat up, obviously prepared for serious conversation. I had been thinking hard about Pauline's comments and was considering how I might best put an end to the relationship without deeply wounding Derek. He, however, began to speak first.

"I know this is going to hurt," he said.

I could not imagine what was going to hurt. He had already done his usual poking about, and it was clear that he was not about to launch into that again. In fact, he had pulled the sheet up over his lower body with uncharacteristic modesty.

I waited expectantly.

"Bathsheba and I are going to give it another try," he said.

Once again I found myself jolted. I had not had an inkling that he was on better terms with Bathsheba. It's true that I hadn't heard him inveigh against her for the past few weeks, but I had put this down to simple fatigue with going over the same material again and again. Now that I thought back on it, however, I realized that he had cancelled our usual Saturday outing with the boys for two weeks in a row, saying that he wanted to spend more time alone with them for bonding purposes. I should have been suspicious, given the difficulty he seemed to have keeping one boy, much less two, from running out into heavy traffic or getting lost for hours in sporting goods stores. I can only assume that I was in a protracted state of obliviousness, a state necessary for me to have continued on in the relationship for as long as I already had.

It now appeared that Derek's time spent bonding with the boys had also been time spent re-bonding with Bathsheba, and that this had led to the reconciliation. Pondering this, I had to admit that there was some logic to it. Derek had grown fractionally better in the parenting role, if only because I had shouldered some of the burden, thereby prolonging his endurance. Bathsheba must have noticed this and realized that taking him back might improve her own situation.

"You're actually responsible, in a way, for bringing us back together," said Derek, affirming my supposition. "When you asked me a while ago whether Bathsheba had help with the boys, it got me thinking about how difficult that job is and how well she's doing with it, which I never really appreciated before. I told her, and she was grateful to hear it."

So there it was. I had played peacemaker between these two warring parties. In truth, there was a certain satisfaction in knowing that I had opened Derek's eyes to his wife's sacrifice and also that I was now rid of him, given what Pauline had pointed out concerning the procreative future of our relationship. Still, it didn't do much for my self-esteem to have him break up with me, especially as he had seen fit to engage in his lackluster lovemaking before relaying the news.

I therefore told him that I was glad to hear that he was getting back with his wife, that it was a relief not to have to spend any more time with his bratty kids, and that also he should know he was lousy in bed. I then told him to go home, and I didn't even back down when he asked if he could spend the night on the pullout couch. I sent him off, even though it was 1 A.M. and raining.

I was called the next morning by Pauline. She said that she had heard how hurt I was by Derek's revelation, but that I should remember what she'd said about his not wanting more children. It seems she had known that Derek was entertaining the idea of going back to his wife, which only made me feel worse, given that, had I been more tuned into what was going on, I would have had the chance to save face and break up with him first.

"He's a big A-hole," I told her.

"I'm sure he is," she reassured me. "But you know, it was hitting below the belt to say those things about his kids. They had nothing to do with it. I know you're hurting, but the kids are innocent bystanders." Derek had apparently relayed to her the details of our conversation.

I told Pauline I *wasn't* hurting, and his kids *were* brats. Yet even as I said it, I began to weep.

"There, there," said Pauline. To her credit, she seemed genuinely concerned. "I didn't want to tell you this before—but he's not worth crying about."

"I know," I whimpered. "It's just that I'll miss his kids." I don't know why I said this, having made it clear that I couldn't stand them, but it kind of slipped out. But, let's face it, it was true. The kids were not mine and a big pain in the ass and had probably already forgotten they had ever met me. But I'd grown fond of both of them—especially Josh, given all the sugar highs we'd shared together. It was, according to Eleanor, another sign of that incorrigible maternal instinct that drew me to the little shits like a moth to the flame. "It's in the genes," she explained. "Thank God I'm a mutation." Eleanor is actually a rather kindhearted person, but she is not, as noted, susceptible to what she terms "kiddie charm." She believes that such susceptibility, like the first high you get from crack cocaine, is what causes so many women to marry jerks and then lose all their brain cells while engaged in the mothering racket. And that's pretty much a direct quote.

Pauline, however, being deeply invested in said mothering racket, couldn't help but be moved by my inadvertent confession. "Oh, Suzanne," she said. "I'm so sorry. You are such an exceptional and loving person. I know you'll find someone better than Derek to be the father of your children."

It was ridiculous, but I felt a welling of gratitude. This was the nicest thing anyone had said about me since my father died, if you don't count what Dr. Chitturi says once a week, which I don't, since I pay her $200 an hour to say it. I also happened to like Pauline's phrasing—she wasn't saying I would find Mr. Darcy to father my children, just "someone better than Derek," which was the sort of modest, realistic statement I could believe in. From a cost-benefit analysis, Pauline's words made me feel momentarily better. OK, I had lost a set of surrogate kids and a boyfriend with a taste for ethnic food—but I had gained a friend.

CHAPTER

5

ALTHOUGH PAULINE'S WORDS had soothed me momentarily, they couldn't entirely keep me from being depressed. I had wasted a lot of time while my biological clock was ticking, only to be rejected by someone I didn't even like. I suppose it would have been more traumatic had I liked Derek, but again, comparative thinking will only get you so far. My self-esteem had taken a nose dive, which isn't good when the baseline for your self-esteem is already pretty low.

Fortunately, I had my Monday morning appointment with Dr. Chitturi to help me through this. One of the immutable features of my life for the past three years has been my Monday morning appointments with Dr. Chitturi.

I should point out that I am no stranger to therapists, having frequented them on and off ever since I suffered from mild bulimia in the ninth grade. But one thing notable about my particular brand of mental illness is that it is low grade. I mean I did throw up after meals in high school for a while, but I couldn't keep doing it; I just didn't have that kind of drive. I also tried cutting myself for a few months in college, but only because my roommate did it and I didn't want her to feel that I was judging her. Yes, I have issues with my mother, but I can't say I hate her the way I hate, say, Hitler or Osama bin Laden. It's true that she is an extremely annoying person who brings out the worst in me (because, let's face it, I want desperately to please her and never feel I can, to paraphrase Dr. Chitturi)—but I'd be lying if I said she didn't mean well and didn't think that everything she was doing was for me—a particularly toxic brand of selflessness that many mothers appear to have perfected.

Also, although I've thought about death, mostly fantasizing about some of the nice things people would say about me at my funeral, I have never seriously contemplated suicide. This is not only because I'm lazy and somewhat cowardly, but also because I'm just not miserable enough. I've been pretty miserable, sure, but not *that* miserable. There have been times when I've wished I could give myself that little shove into extreme misery so that I'd get to spend a few months in a nice facility where they have yoga classes and soft-spoken nurses who give you medication in little paper cups. But, try as I may, my misery has never been acute enough to win me these sorts of perks.

As a result of my low-grade mental illness, most of the therapists I've seen haven't taken me very seriously. They took my money, but I always thought they were in cahoots with my mother and felt I ought to pull myself together and stop bellyaching.

Dr. Chitturi, however, was different, which is why I've been with her for so long. "Your mother is a very narcissistic woman, Suzanne," she tells me at almost every session. "She has done a lot of damage to your sensitive psyche." Hearing Dr. Chitturi say this always puts me in a better mood. You'd think that I wouldn't have to pay an arm and a leg to hear someone say what I already know every week for three years, but that's how therapy works.

Dr. Chitturi's appearance also has a soothing effect on my nerves. She wears saris and has one of those dots on her forehead, a look that somehow works for me, don't ask me why. I once caught a glimpse of her in the supermarket and she was wearing sweat pants and a tee shirt and her face was dot-less, which made me think that maybe she dresses up only for our sessions. This disturbed me a little until I realized that even if it's true, I don't care. When you go to a therapist you want the production values. Dr. Chitturi, in addition to the saris and the dot, has colorful cushions with little mirrors sewn into them and uses an air freshener that smells like incense. I like the whole package, and the only problem is that she's a psychologist, not a psychiatrist, which, if you know anything about these things, means that for medication I have to see someone else. It's a pain-in-the-ass division of labor, just another instance where the system seems designed to make you nuts—only in this case, you're *already* nuts.

Fortunately for me, Eleanor happens to have accumulated a practically endless supply of antidepressants and anxiety meds during her divorce from the sociopathic Ronnie, a hedge fund manager discovered to be involved in more than the run-of-the-mill illegalities common among his peers. Eleanor, who had realized early on that Ronnie was a mistake but hadn't bothered to do anything about it for years, had finally gotten up the energy to leave him after his name was published in the papers and he started getting death threats from former clients. It was during this difficult patch that she accumulated said pharmaceutical collection, of which I have since become the beneficiary. Dr. Chitturi would probably chastise me in her pleasant singsong voice if she knew I was medicating myself ("Suzanne, it is not a good thing; you could make a very large mistake"), but I have not seen fit to tell her.

The day after Derek broke it to me that he was returning to Bathsheba, I immediately made an early morning run over to Eleanor's to forage for Xanax in her medicine chest. The Xanax calmed me down enough to get a few hours of fitful sleep that night. But it had worn off by the time of my appointment Monday morning, and I presented myself in Dr. Chitturi's office looking properly unhinged.

"You appear to be very agitated today, Suzanne," said Dr. Chitturi when I plopped down on her sofa with its mirrored cushions. "Please feel free to tell me about it." Dr. Chitturi talks this way, which gives me the sense that what I have to say actually carries some weight. For me, style is everything in therapy, and, as a result, I always get a lift from the way Dr. Chitturi expresses what seems like genuine interest in what is bothering me, even though I am paying her $200 an hour to do so.

"I must conclude that you had a particularly difficult weekend," continued Dr. Chitturi. One of the reasons I schedule my appointments on Mondays is that I invariably have a difficult weekend, though this one, as she noted, was particularly difficult. "Tell me about your distress," she urged sympathetically.

Again, Dr. Chitturi had hit the nail on the head. Derek was my distress, and just getting this called by the right name made me feel better already. I told Dr. Chitturi that Derek had broken up with me and was going back to his wife.

"But you did not like this man," noted Dr. Chitturi, sounding puzzled. "The last time we talked you said you were going to end this relationship."

"I know I did," I moaned plaintively, "but I wanted to do the breaking up. It makes me feel like a miserable loser to have him break up with me."

"Suzanne," said Dr. Chitturi, fastening her benign gaze on me with a certain severity, "you are *not* a loser. You are a very caring and compassionate person who did not want to hurt this unpleasant man's feelings."

This was a version of what Pauline had said, and hearing it from two people in two days was definitely nice. I also liked her point about my not wanting to hurt Derek's feelings. Dr. Chitturi is always putting this kind of good spin on things, so that instead of feeling like a miserable loser, I feel more like Mother Teresa. This time was no exception. I felt like a caring and compassionate person for about half an hour after I left Dr. Chitturi's office—and then I went back to feeling like a miserable loser again.

CHAPTER

6

THE QUESTION FACING ME now was what I should do next. I had wasted a lot of time dating Derek, but then, what does that mean: "wasted a lot of time"? "Do not think in those terms, Suzanne," cautioned Dr. Chitturi, "nothing in life is a waste of time."

This was a good point. Hadn't I decided to moderate my expectations, which would include factoring in the occasional disastrous interlude of the sort I had just experienced with Derek? Hadn't I chucked my search for Mr. Darcy and recalibrated my sense of what was reasonable to expect out of life? I would therefore look at my foray with Derek as a test run, a preliminary voyage. If my apartment building was going to serve as a microcosm of the great world, why should I expect to make a worthwhile discovery right away? Hadn't Columbus done a lot of sailing around in those ships and sucking up to that queen before he made it to America?

The episode with Derek had sent me pretty far off course—to continue the above, admittedly strained, metaphor—but who knows what new continent might float into view now that I had broken up with him? (Technically, of course, I didn't break up with Derek; Derek broke up with me. But since it was my *intention* to break up with him, and his beating me to it really, really depresses me, I have decided to refer to the breakup as my doing.) Some good things had come in the course of my maiden voyage: I had made a friend in Pauline and gotten to know some of the other playground mothers. That was something.

So here I was, determined to continue my search for a life despite the initial blip I had encountered in my efforts. Since my aim was not to stray too far from home, I proceeded to consult the bulletin board in the mailroom of my building. I guess that what I was after was an announcement of some sort that would lead me, if not to a new world, at least to some distraction from the old one.

The mailroom is a cramped space behind the periodically present doorman Pedro's desk, where mail is mis-delivered on a regular basis. A large bulletin board above the mailboxes is festooned with notices. Some of these are for mundane services: a discount at the new dry cleaners or a free appetizer at the new Italian restaurant, both establishments trying valiantly to distinguish themselves from the other dry cleaners and Italian restaurants on the Upper West Side. There are also the ratty-looking flyers with snip-off numbers at the bottom where people in the building announce their desire to sell a car, a computer, a sofa bed, or a complete set of Wedgwood china, serves 12, never used—which, from what Pedro tells me, is the fallout from the divorce in 7C. A standard notice on the board is for the area's craft fairs. You'd think that Upper West Siders, given how many of us live in apartments the size of shoeboxes, would avoid craft fairs, a prime locale for the acquisition of overpriced things we don't need. But the appetite for crafts in this part of the city is unquenchable. I myself, in a moment of craft-fair weakness, recently purchased a hand-carved walking stick made from indigenous wood that I now keep propped near my front door in case anyone has a sudden need for support in getting across the room. (I unfortunately misplaced the tag made from recycled waste products, explaining what country the wood in the walking stick is indigenous to, reducing its value as a conversation piece, if not its usefulness for those who need help traversing the twenty-foot expanse of my apartment.)

Anyway, I ignored the craft fairs et al. and concentrated instead on the more practical notices relating to the building. Among these were announcements for a Weight Watchers meeting, a divorced fathers session, and a healthy prostate information session, to be held in various apartments in the building in the course of the week. None of these meetings, needless to say, could I in good conscience attend—or even in bad, being incapable of passing for an overweight woman or a divorced, prostate-concerned man.

One day, however, a posting appeared announcing a meeting for dog owners. Billed as a Doggie Meet and Greet, it was being convened so that the management could address the stench of urine in the elevator that had become a chronic problem. I knew this because Pedro, the periodic doorman, had explained it when I mentioned the unpleasant odor. Obviously, dogs too had prostate problems.

The notice asked all dog owners to meet for a short information session in the lobby. Treats and doggie neckerchiefs would be distributed, after which everyone would proceed to Riverside Park for a festive run and fetch.

This sounded like just the sort of gathering that might serve my purposes. Dog owners are prone to be humane and responsible people, both qualities that I respect, even if I do not possess them myself. Perhaps this group would yield a soul mate, or, barring that, at least open me to the pleasures of the canine world.

Admittedly, I did not own a dog, but this did not strike me as a major impediment. I could acquire one. I even stood for a few minutes in front of the pet shop on Broadway wondering if I would be charmed by one of the bleary-eyed puppies lolling inside their little boxes. A depressed-looking beagle looked promising until he began licking his private parts. This was just as well. I am not a very neat person, and a dog might cause me to pitch headlong into full fledged squalor. Besides, when you've lived alone in a studio apartment in Manhattan without owning much of anything, you're going to think twice about owning something that's alive.

So, after concluding that acquiring a dog of my own wasn't really a good idea, I decided to borrow one. As it happens, within the category of dogs available for me to borrow, there existed exactly one: Eleanor's wheaten terrier.

Eleanor, despite being unsusceptible to kiddie charm is enormously susceptible to doggie charm. This apparent inconsistency, in my experience, is not uncommon. People who like dogs want a level of control that children are never going to give them. At the time Eleanor acquired Wordsworth (as the dog is, with whimsical pretension, named), she had just separated from the sociopathic Ronnie. This meant that Wordsworth came off well, being nicer and more intelligent than Ronnie—which isn't saying much.

The wheaten breed has the following credentials that, for a brief interval, made it a popular choice among a certain segment of the New York City population: it doesn't shed and can therefore be billed as hypoallergenic, and it has an exotic pedigree related to sheepherding in Ireland—Ireland seeming to New Yorkers the sort of place they would never want to live but is good for a dog to come from. Wheatens are also cute in a Disney-ish sort of way. You see a wheaten, even if it has that ridiculous wheaten cut that you know the dog hates, and you think, He looks like he's out of a Disney movie.

The reason wheatens have since sunk in popularity is because the breed has several downsides, which become noticeable only after you've plunked down the fifteen hundred dollars it costs to purchase one and framed the pedigree with all the Irish ancestors in a place of honor in the kitchen. Here's what you discover: Wheatens have delicate stomachs, are extremely stubborn, and require full-time maintenance or their Disney-esque hair will knot into unmanageable frizz and have to be shaved off, making them look less Disney-ish and more Holocaust-ish. Eleanor's wheaten's stomach problems had ruined her Abyssinian rug and cost her a fortune in vet bills, and the hair problem had indentured her to a groomer on York Avenue. But, in the manner common among New Yorkers whose appetite for abuse is bottomless, she only loved the dog all the more.

When I asked to borrow Wordsworth, therefore, she was initially skittish.

"I don't know," she said.

"It would only be for a few days. It might help me turn my life around."

As you may have guessed by now, it was my idea to go to the Doggie Meet and Greet, claiming Wordsworth's owner was on vacation and that I needed help caring for him. This, I believed, would establish a connection with another dog owner, presumably a single and attractive man with a good job and an apartment bigger than mine, that could be cultivated once Wordsworth had been returned.

"But he needs to be walked four times a day," said Eleanor, surveying me doubtfully.

I said that walking Wordsworth would not be a problem. What else did I have to do anyway, except sit around the house writing press releases about indoor air quality?

"But you'd have to get dressed." Eleanor knew about my tendency to stay in my nightgown until I got hungry enough to have to run out to the Korean market.

I assured her that my habits had changed. I now got dressed on a regular basis—and half of New York walks their dogs in their pajamas anyway.

"But grooming," said Eleanor. "I can't see you brushing him."

"You don't brush him either," I noted. This was true, which is why the groomer on York Avenue was always yelling at her.

"But I'm the owner," she explained. "I'm allowed to backslide. If you borrow him you have to brush him."

"So I'll brush him," I said.

She brought out the various brushes and detanglers. Also a very large nail clipper. "You need to keep his nails trimmed," she explained.

"OK," I lied.

"But be careful not to cut him," she said. "It'll freak him out. He's afraid of blood."

"I'll be careful."

"And keep the TV low. Loud noises upset him. But he likes sitcoms; the laugh track relaxes him."

I told her I loved sitcoms.

"Wordsworth eats only dry kibble," she continued, "which makes things easy—unless he starts throwing up. Then, you need to boil rice and add some chicken bouillon. Under no circumstances are you to feed him filet mignon."

"Why would I feed him filet mignon?"

"I'm just saying. He likes it, but it doesn't agree with him."

I told her everything would be followed to the letter. Dog people, I figured, were nuts and thus bound to exaggerate. How hard could it be take care of a dog for a few days? I had managed Derek's kids, no easy feat, so taking care of a wheaten terrier would be a piece of cake. He wasn't even that big, and he'd just been to the groomer, so he had a fluffy, amiable look. He was now jumping around in a friendly way, which suggested that he liked me.

"Think of it," I noted, "he'll get used to me and then you can have someone to leave him with when you go away." This was the principal difficulty Eleanor had faced since the acquisition of Wordsworth. The last time she had gone on vacation—for a post-divorce rest cure at Kripalu, the austere but extravagantly priced spa in the Berkshires—she had left the dog with her parents, who had fed him the toxic filet mignon.

"I love this dog," I said, as Wordsworth jumped up on me, getting paw marks on my white blouse and making a snag in my wool skirt. "I'm not generally crazy about dogs, but I've always had a special feeling for Wordsworth."

Saying this apparently did the trick. Dog owners have something of the vanity of parents and believe your praise, no matter how excessive or absurd it is. They are especially susceptible to the idea that their dog has a unique appeal, something, they secretly believe, which lifts the dog to the level of an honorary human being. Thus, when I noted my special feeling for Wordsworth, Eleanor acquiesced, and he was transferred to me with all his accoutrements (kibble, brushes, leashes, bowls, etc.). He proceeded to bound happily with me out of the apartment as Eleanor looked on with doting concern from the doorway.

Outside, Wordsworth peed near the tree on the corner of Lexington and 70th and crapped in front of the Sonia Rykiel store on Madison that was, I had been advised, his favorite spot. I was now hoping to get him across Central Park so I could make it back to my apartment for a nap before the Doggie Meet and Greet, but that was when Wordsworth decided he'd had enough of me and wanted to go home.

"No, Wordsworth," I said, as he pulled in the direction of Eleanor's building, "you're spending a few days with me."

But Wordsworth would have none of it. He is not a big dog, but he does weigh fifty pounds and is well muscled owing to the fact that his ancestors herded sheep somewhere on the Irish heath. I, moreover, had my hands full with the poop bag and the doggie accoutrements. I tried my best to pull him in the direction of the park, while he pulled in the direction of Eleanor's building, and we continued in this tug of war for a while until I finally realized it was hopeless and hailed a cab.

Fortunately, Wordsworth jumped happily into the cab— he likes cabs, I later learned, because they usually mean that Eleanor is taking him to visit her parents in Brooklyn, where he hopes for filet mignon. But once we arrived in front of my apartment and he realized that it wasn't the Park Slope home of the Feldmans, he refused to get out. I pulled and he pulled back, gluing himself to the far corner of the cab.

"Lady," said the driver, after two potential fares had wandered away, "I'm going to have to put the meter back on if you don't get the goddamn dog out of here."

The thought of the meter running gave me a rush of adrenaline, and I yanked Wordsworth out onto the curb, where he slouched down in a mean, stubborn crouch until Pedro, the periodic doorman, came out, lifted him up, and carried him into the elevator. Once we got to my floor, I dragged him through the hall as he squatted on his haunches, his nails making a screeching sound on the laminated wood.

When I finally maneuvered him into my apartment, I went into the kitchen and consumed the Mars bar that I had been carefully whittling away for the past few days. I then stretched out on the couch and fell asleep, while Wordsworth watched some sitcom reruns (*According to Jim*, *The King of Queens*) until it was time to go to the Doggie Meet and Greet at 4 P.M.

I had dreaded trying to get Wordsworth out of the apartment, but this didn't prove to be a problem. He leapt joyously out the door, thinking, I suppose, that he was returning to Eleanor. It would be getting him back in that would be a challenge, but I decided to think about that later.

We descended to the lobby, where the dogs and their owners had congregated. Not being a dog person, seeing lots of dogs together in a small space makes me nervous. Where dog people are likely to think, "Look at all those adorable dogs," I think, "Look at all those dogs that could, if so inclined, tear me limb for limb."

As soon as we entered the lobby, Wordsworth began growling, though not at me. He didn't trust the other dogs either. I have to say I felt a kinship with him. I know that it takes a lot of time for people to warm up to me, if in fact they ever do, and Wordsworth seemed to feel the same way. Here were all these other dogs, prancing around, jumping up on their owners, sniffing happily at each others' butts. And here *he* was, knowing no one and being totally out of it. It made him feel bad about himself, which made him growl, which made the owners of the other dogs pull their dogs away from him, which made him feel worse, etc. etc. It was the sort of feedback loop that I was familiar with and that Dr. Chitturi was trying to break me out of.

I noticed a large greyhound giving Wordsworth the once-over and a boxer whose eyes were bulging at him nastily. Wordsworth saw this, too, and began straining at his leash and baring his teeth. He didn't look too cute now, and I wondered if it might have helped if Eleanor had given him one of those wheaten cuts, since a foolish-looking haircut can do a lot to defuse a dog's menace. But Wordsworth just had a lot of hair, and it had begun to look a little matted as a result of the struggle he'd put up getting out of the cab and into my apartment. He had gone, in other words, from looking like a Disney-ish dog to looking kind of funky and dissipated.

Two irritatingly cute bichons had been scooped up by their owners, a large middle-aged couple who were wearing pink bandannas that matched the ones around their dogs' necks. "Don't let the big dog scare you," they said loudly to the bichons they were cradling protectively in their arms, "he's just a big old bully. Mommy and daddy will protect you." This made me want to bite them myself. For one thing, I hate people who refer to themselves as their dogs' mommy and daddy. And for another, Wordsworth was not a big dog; he was a medium-sized dog of high quality—he'd cost Eleanor fifteen hundred dollars.

Meanwhile, another yapping bichon began showing off by scuttling in very close to Wordsworth and then running away. Wordsworth tried to snap at this dog, only to find that it had scurried out of range, which caused him to lunge in the direction of where it had been. I pulled the leash back with both hands, but the little dog was making it hard. His owner, a short bald man for whom the dog's behavior was clearly a form of compensatory aggression, egged him on: "Isn't she a spunky little girl?" he said, looking around him proudly. "Show the big dog you're not afraid."

I was pulling on Wordsworth now with all my strength, trying to keep him from breaking loose and wreaking havoc, when I noticed Stephen, the wispy math teacher who had been at Pauline's book group, standing near the front door with a golden retriever puppy. It was cute, and a circle of other dog owners were admiring it in the extravagant manner characteristic of dog people. I could see that Stephen had recognized me, had registered my distress, and was trying to extricate himself from the puppy lovers to help me out. I felt a momentary welling of gratitude for this kindness. But before he could wrest his dog away from the fawning circle, someone else was at my elbow, taking the leash from my hand and, with a firm yank, bringing Wordsworth to heel.

Needless to say, I was relieved. I had genuinely feared that Wordsworth was about to get away from me and would consequently either lose his life or be severely disabled, with the result that Eleanor would never forgive me, so that not only would I end up a wizened spinster, but I wouldn't even have a best girlfriend anymore to go out to dinner with and complain to. But now, thankfully, I wouldn't have to worry about the not-going-out-to-dinner-and-complaining part.

I looked up to see who had rescued me and, let me tell you, the breath practically left my body. Really, if I were going to sketch a knight in shining armor as he might appear on the Upper West Side of Manhattan at a Doggie Meet and Greet, he would look like this guy. He was about my age, tall, well built, with a head of luxurious black hair and a pair of sparkling blue eyes. I'm not exaggerating when I say "luxurious" and "sparkling." I know that these adjectives don't usually apply in real life, but in this case, they did.

"You looked like you needed a little help," said this fictional-appearing creature. "I have experience with the breed." He pointed to his own dog, a wheaten—I'm not making this up—though his was a well-behaved one, perhaps because he had the foolish wheaten cut. "This is Longfellow," he said.

The fact that both his dog and mine had the names of dead white male poets might seem like a startling coincidence, but this was the Upper West Side of Manhattan, where, though it is politically incorrect to, say, write a dissertation on such figures, it is almost required to name your dog after them. Longfellow, though named after the lesser of the two poets, was definitely the better behaved. He had a mellow, accepting look about him, and gazed pleasantly at Wordsworth as though he had known him all his life.

As Longfellow appraised Wordsworth, I now had a chance to do the same with my rescuer. Let me officially report that he resembled—and again I'm not exaggerating—the young Sean Connery. Why hadn't I seen him in the building before? How could I have missed such a paragon wandering in my vicinity? As I was now in the hands of a benign fate, the subject of my musings seemed to intuit my thoughts.

"I'm Philip," he explained. "I just moved here from Chicago."

I was looking up at him with my mouth open, and for a moment, I confess, I forgot my own name. I've forgotten things before under stressful circumstances: my zip code, what year it is, the name of the vice president of the United States. But I have never been so rattled as to forget my own name. This was a first, an indication of how dazzling this specimen of masculinity was.

"I'm Suzanne," I finally summoned up. "This isn't really my dog. I'm taking care of him for a friend." It seemed important to get this out of the way so as to make room for more salient details related to, say, the china pattern I wanted to register for our wedding.

Before we could talk more, however, there was an interruption by the building manager to address the urination-in-the-elevator problem. "If it continues, we might be forced to take dire measures," he warned.

This elicited a wave of distress from those present. "Dire measures"—what could that mean? There were stifled gasps and some attempt at protest.

"The dog who did it probably isn't even here," said one of the bandanna-wearing bichon owners huffily.

"That's not my problem," said the manager. "I can't run a building when dogs pee in the elevator. It has to stop."

No one dared ask what would happen if it didn't, but there was some whispered speculation on the subject

"They could banish dogs from the building," Philip murmured in my ear. "In my old co-op they did that. We had to move." He looked down fondly at Longfellow.

"You could install a camera," called out the wispy Stephen.

Everyone, including the manager, agreed that this was a good idea.

"Problem solved," I said, smiling up at Philip.

"Not necessarily," said Philip soberly. "The small dogs can be very sly about how they do it. Just dribbling, you know. Even the big dogs don't always lift a leg. It might be hard to tell."

I could hear others around us discussing the peeing techniques of various dogs that might circumvent the camera. But the manager had moved on to address the subject of barking. "Three complaints and we will have to ask you to make other arrangements for your pet," said the manager. I was pleased to see everyone look severely at the short bald man whose bichon was yapping wildly.

"I see you gave Longfellow the wheaten cut," I noted to Philip, as the barking issue was discussed. We didn't have to listen to this part of the discussion given that wheatens are quiet dogs and tend to growl rather than bark.

"We know it's a little foolish but we like it," said Philip fondly.

The use of the first person plural for the second time gave me pause. Was he simply enmeshed with his dog or was he—my heart sank at the thought—already taken?

"Are you married?" I asked, deciding to be direct, but trying to sound nonchalant, despite my trepidation.

To my relief, Philip shook his head adamantly. "But I'd like to be," he said. "And I hope to. . . ." His voice trailed off, wistfully.

Could there be a better answer? How many men, especially men who look like the young Sean Connery, would tell you that they longed to get married? Not many, I assure you.

"Me too," I agreed. Wasn't it great that I could admit my desire openly after only five minutes of meeting this Adonis?

He looked at me excitedly. "It's awful, isn't it? It's been *so* hard."

I said I agreed it was hard, but I have to admit I was surprised: I could understand how it was hard for me, but not how it was hard for him. (For readers who may be ahead of me here, please be indulgent—I was bedazzled.)

"You should come to dinner tomorrow," Philip now followed briskly.

Was it possible? Could it be that here in the lobby of my apartment building, my ship had finally come in? Normally, I had to grow on people, but the young Sean Connery apparently had, in a few minutes, made a survey of my character and found it to his liking. He had told me he wanted to get married; he had invited me to dinner. My mother had always said that when it's right, it's easy.

The building manager had ended the information session, having duly frightened all the dog owners and given them fodder for weeks of serious discussion. He then handed our dog treats and refrigerator magnets advertising an appliance store in Brooklyn owned by his brother-in-law. Most of the owners immediately jettisoned the biscuits as insufficiently nutritious ("doggie junk food," I heard someone mutter), but I happen to like junk food and so I let Wordsworth gobble up his treat. He probably would have eaten Longfellow's too had Philip not quickly but discreetly deposited it in the trash can near the front door as we went out.

The information session concluded, we all made our way to the dog run in Riverside Park to decompress. I was floating on air. Philip walked beside me chatting about the habits of wheatens and then segueing into a discussion of his work. He was an architect and had already, since his move from Chicago, acquired several excellent commissions, including one for an addition to the Brooklyn Museum.

An architect doing an addition to the Brooklyn Museum! This was so easy, he must be the one, I thought. My mother, who had never, to my knowledge, been right before in her life, must finally have emerged from her thirty-four-year slump.

I told him I was a technical writer and gave him some humorous nuggets about the air-conditioning engineers. He laughed, a good sign.

Stephen, the wispy math teacher, had, meanwhile, come up on my other side, determined to talk, even though he must have seen that I was deep into discussion with my Prince Charming.

"I saw you were having a little trouble with your dog," he said. "But you're OK now?" He looked at Wordsworth and glanced at Philip.

"Yes," I said with the mock graciousness that comes of being under the protection of someone who looks like the young Sean Connery. "All fine now. This is Philip. And you're . . . ?"

I hadn't forgotten his name, but I felt that appearing to have forgotten gave me a breezy, glamorous look—as though I met so many people in my busy life that I couldn't possibly be expected to keep them straight.

"Stephen Danziger," he said with a mixture of amusement and good nature that took some of the edge off my glamorous pose. Philip said hello, then proceeded to become involved in feeding treats to Wordsworth and Longfellow (these treats, apparently, of a more high-end variety than those that the building manager had distributed).

"You missed the discussion of Proust," Stephen remarked.

I have neglected to mention that I had taken a hiatus from book club after the breakup with Derek. Even Pauline had agreed that it might be a chore for me to sit through a discussion of *Swann's Way* with Derek and Bathsheba present. It was typical of Derek to bring Bathsheba back into book club even though he knew that I was a member and might feel uncomfortable. This was not a malevolent gesture on his part, I acknowledge, only a thoughtless one, reinforcing what you probably already suspect: Derek, though very sensitive with regard to his own feelings, has no sensitivity whatsoever with regard to other people's. This paradox is commonly encountered among the citizens of New York— behavior that I, on occasion, happen to share.

"I can't say the reconciliation is a good thing for book group," Pauline had informed me on the subject of Derek and Bathsheba after the Proust session. "I used to think Bathsheba made good comments, but I have to revise my judgment; she's really very pretentious and controlling." I admit that I appreciated the loyalty behind this observation and took some comfort in imagining Bathsheba pontificating while the rest of book club rolled its eyes.

"I'm taking a break from book club," I blithely explained to Stephen now. "I thought Pauline told everyone."

"She just said you had something to do that evening."

"Actually, for a while," I corrected. "I'm just too busy right now to fit it in." I should note that I am always being told by other people that they are "too busy" to do this or that, a source of mystification to me, since I am never busy at all. Thus, it was a consolation to finally be in a position to tell someone else that I was too busy.

"That's too bad," he said. "I liked your observation about diapers in *Moby Dick*."

He was smiling, and I realized that he was referring to the discussion about children in *The Great Gatsby* that had resulted in a brief riff between us—and I have to say that I was momentarily taken aback by his having remembered something I'd said that wasn't even witty. Most of the time, men don't listen to me when I speak, much less remember what I said weeks after the fact.

I looked at Stephen now, flattered by his retentiveness. He had a thin, earnest face and slightly bloodshot eyes, but he wasn't exactly bad-looking and not really wispy, despite my having thought of him this way since having first encountered him. As you may have noticed, I have a tendency to make snap judgments about people, often based on evidence that exists purely in my own imagination. Stephen's wispiness was a case in point. His hair was thinning a bit, to be sure, but it was neatly combed and not unattractive in color or texture. In general, he had a nice way about him, and I momentarily recalled that Pauline had had him, not Derek, in mind for me to begin with. But all this was of no relevance now. Even though I'd convinced myself that looking for Mr. Darcy was a fruitless goal, one to be dropped in the interest of my mental health, I now felt that I had been premature in dropping it and that I should reinstate it. Philip, along with resembling the young Sean Connery, also looked a bit like Laurence Olivier, who had played Mr. Darcy in the old Hollywood movie of *Pride and Prejudice*. With someone of this caliber so obviously smitten and asking me to dinner, let's face it, an ordinary man like Stephen is going to look pretty shoddy.

And so I gave Stephen one of those exaggerated smiles that mean "you're dismissed now," and which some particularly dim-witted men don't pick up on. But Stephen, to his credit, got it right away. He moved off, and his golden retriever puppy immediately attracted a new circle of admirers. I could see that he was not in the best spirits, and I suppose I understood, having been there myself numerous times. But hey, I'd suffered rejection and humiliation at the hands of the opposite sex; shouldn't I have the chance to make someone else suffer these things? I know that it's this kind of thinking that perpetuates the world's abuse, but I couldn't help it; I was feeling heady in the presence of the young Sean Connery, and my moral sense had gone out the window. Or, to put it in the context of the occasion: it's a dog-eat-dog world; get over it.

Once Philip had finished giving out the doggie treats—Longfellow, I noted, did a variety of tricks for his, while Wordsworth watched, feeling what I imagined to be a sense of his own inadequacy—he returned to my side and began pointing out details of the architectural facades on Riverside Drive. I'd always wanted to talk architecture this way—it gives you a savvy New York look to be walking beside someone who knows a lot about pediments and lintels. Philip and I gazed up at the buildings together, our heads practically touching, the two dogs trotting happily beside us. It was idyllic, and I could already foresee the years stretching ahead, walking hand in hand, looking at the facades of memorable buildings, Longfellow ambling alongside the stroller.

I am vain enough to admit that it even crossed my mind that someone who looked like Philip would father nice-looking children—children who would be able to bypass the Kaplan nose (which, if this is giving you some ideas about me, I happen to have mostly avoided myself). But even though I dodged that bullet, the genes are there on *both* sides (my dad's grandfather got "Davis" from an impatient immigration officer at Ellis Island unwilling to spell "Davidowitz"). Clearly you want to have something strong to counteract the possibility of those genes rearing their head—or, as it were, their nose.

After the run was over and we headed back, Wordsworth, lulled by the lively example of Longfellow, was compliant, and I had no trouble entering the building and getting in the elevator with him.

"Don't forget dinner tomorrow," said Philip, kissing my cheek. "We're having pistachio-crusted tilapia with a tomato coulis."

I looked at him and Longfellow with bemusement. It was nice to love your dog, but that degree of anthropomorphizing was a bit much. I'd have to break him of the habit after we were married.

CHAPTER

7

ELEANOR CALLED the next day saying she wanted Wordsworth back.

"I'm miserable," she explained. "Every time I'm about to go out, I reach for his leash. I even miss hearing him whine at night." Wordsworth, I neglected to report, suffers from night terrors. At around 2 A.M. he begins thrashing and whimpering, and you have to give him some chicken bouillon and have him listen to Bruce Springsteen for a while before he calms down. To be honest, I couldn't bear the thought of another night with him. But I could see how, for Eleanor, who had lived for ten years with Ronnie, a sociopath with a mix of sadistic and regressive tendencies, Wordsworth's doggie neurosis might seem soothing.

"I know I said you could have him for a few days, but Ronnie's been calling, wanting to get back together. I need all the moral support I can get right now."

I knew she was expecting me to put up a fight, but as I saw it, Wordsworth had already done his work. If he was a deeply neurotic dog, he was also, for my purposes, an extremely efficient one. I was prepared to return him, only I wasn't going to miss getting some credit for it.

"But I've just had him for one day," I said in a plaintive tone.

"I know, and I'm sorry," sympathized Eleanor, who probably thought that I'd grown as attached to Wordsworth as she was. "But I *have* to have him back."

I gave a heavy, theatrical sigh. "OK," I said. "You can come get him—if you must."

"You're the best," said Eleanor. "I won't forget this. I know I owe you big time."

It was nice to rack up some points here, especially since Eleanor's assets had recently greatly increased. It seems that Ronnie, in an effort to elude the long arm of the law, had transferred a chunk of his savings to Eleanor's account, and she had rationalized this ill-gotten gain as recompense for pain and suffering. I wondered now if the return of Wordsworth could be parlayed into some important item, like a bigger apartment. Hopefully, however, marriage to Philip, a successful architect, would relieve me of all future money worries and I could content myself with a moral advantage rather than a financial one.

"Your mental health is what's important," I said magnanimously.

"You're the best," repeated Eleanor. "You can come over any time if you want to visit Wordsworth."

As I saw it, once I was married to Philip, we'd soon be bonding a lot over the two wheaten terriers. I could foresee many afternoons with Eleanor and me romping with Longfellow and Wordsworth, Philip playing with the dogs and charming both of us, though demonstrating his undying affection for me in particular, with the result that Eleanor would regain her lost belief in the ability of men to be decent.

I could even hear strains of made-for-television-movie music playing in the background.

While I was still enjoying this daydream, Eleanor came for Wordsworth, and I proceeded to spend the rest of the afternoon picking an outfit to wear to dinner with Philip that evening. After trying on everything in my closet and leaving it all inside out on the floor, I finally settled on jeans and a tee shirt—a variation on what I'd worn for the Doggie Meet and Greet. Why mess with a winning formula? When I showed up at Philip's apartment at the appointed hour, I had a bottle of wine and no dog, which might be a disappointment to Longfellow but which I didn't think was likely to bother Philip. His greeting, however, suggested otherwise.

"Where's your friend?" was the first thing he asked when he answered the door. He seemed genuinely dismayed. Had he taken to Wordsworth that much? Dog lovers, I knew, were nuts, so it was possible.

"Oh, his owner took him back," I explained. "She came home from her trip a little earlier than expected."

"But didn't *she* want to come?" he asked, furrowing his impeccable brow. "We wanted to meet her."

I must have looked confused because he gestured behind him, and out of the kitchen, at his summoning, emerged a man in a scarf and an apron. Let me tell you something: If you see a man wearing a scarf indoors, he's probably gay, and if you see a man wearing an apron, he's also probably gay. But if you see a man wearing a scarf and an apron, he is definitely gay. Very gay. This man who came out of the kitchen was, and, as the veil lifted, so, I realized, was Philip. And there was the rebuttal to my mother's maxim, whose infallibility with regard to being wrong now remained unchallenged. When it's easy, that can mean only one thing: he's gay.

For those interested, it was a spectacular dinner—Kurt, Philip's significant other, had spent a year at the Cordon Bleu in Paris, and Philip was an expert on puff pastry. It was the beginning of a beautiful friendship—two beautiful friendships, to be precise. Unfortunately, friendship, beautiful or otherwise, was not what I had had in mind.

CHAPTER

8

So what was I going to do now? I had called Eleanor to discuss the Philip debacle, but she couldn't talk too long because she had to go off to read to the blind. She does this once a week, and that's what got me thinking. Every psychiatrist I've had since I was sixteen has told me to reach out to those less fortunate than myself so as to put my own situation in perspective. But the fact is that I'd never been so inclined. Why, I wonder, doesn't someone reach out to me? Don't I have enough problems to warrant sympathy? It's true that I'm not a Sudanese child soldier or a paraplegic war veteran, but look at what I've been saddled with in the way of a mother! As every psychiatrist I've had since the age of sixteen has also told me, pain is a relative thing, and mental suffering can be as valid and acute as physical suffering. OK, even I know that this is really lame, so please forget I said it.

One of the problems with good works for me is a matter of scale. Whenever I start to think about famine and genocide and just plain meanness in the world, I feel overwhelmed: it's hard to visualize what working to alleviate famine, genocide, and meanness is actually going to look like, especially when you know that there are all these people along the way between me and the famine-stricken who, if they're corrupt, are going to use my donation to buy a villa or a private jet, or, if they're not corrupt and just doing their job, to help pay for the flower arrangements at some big charity gala to raise "serious" money, since the money I could give wouldn't be serious but just enough to pay for maybe one or two centerpieces. If I had loads of money I wouldn't mind giving a truckload of it to one of those charity fundraisers so I could eat a gourmet meal at a table with a nice centerpiece while getting thanked for it. But paying for the centerpiece at one or two tables at a party where I'm not invited—no.

I should point out that at one juncture I did contemplate volunteering at a suicide hotline. I thought it might be interesting work and valuable in the event that I needed its services myself some day. As I noted earlier, I have never seriously contemplated suicide, but that doesn't mean I won't, and working for a suicide hotline seemed like a good precaution, since I'd know who the best volunteers were and could ask for them if I needed to be talked down. But as I considered the idea further, it occurred to me that my reasoning was off. If I knew the people working for the suicide hotline, I'd be too embarrassed to call them, which would defeat the purpose of working there and maybe put me at higher risk for killing myself. So I tabled the idea.

Of course, nothing that I've said so far precludes my doing volunteer work of some other sort, like the kind Eleanor does. You're probably thinking, Why can't you do that, you selfish ——? This is not a bad question, and I am, I admit, a selfish ——, which will only be confirmed when I confess that I'm not motivated enough to do such work. I used to think that something was seriously wrong with me for not being motivated until I came to the conclusion, possibly to appease my sense of guilt, that most people do volunteer work not out of genuine altruism but in order to boast that they do it. I'm convinced that Eleanor, for example, reads to the blind so she can say things like: "I can't have lunch on Thursday; I'm reading to the blind." Then there are all the people I meet who work one evening a week in a soup kitchen—"It's so rewarding peeling all those potatoes, etc., etc."—but if their cleaning woman calls in sick, do you think they'd run over with chicken soup? I don't think so. My cynicism here is, as I noted, based on trying to rationalize why I don't volunteer, so please take it with a grain of salt.

But my new approach to getting a life put things in this area in a new perspective. You may recall that I was taking Jane Austen's "three or four families in a country village" and applying it to my apartment building on West 76th Street. Which is to say, I was trying to think small. Yes, my aim was to get a life, but this also meant helping people who happened to live in *my* country village. It would be easier than going to a soup kitchen across town and more meaningful than handing over a check for a centerpiece. And who knows? It might beef up my social life.

So there I was, suddenly asking Pedro, the periodic doorman, if anyone in the building needed help, explaining that I had time on my hands and wanted to "give back." That was the phrase that I knew you were supposed to use: "how can I give back?" It was unclear what it was I was giving back for. What did I have? An apartment the size of a shoebox in the West 70s and a job working for air-conditioning engineers, but beyond that, not much. But I suppose if you compare me to Sudanese child soldiers and paraplegic war veterans, I had it pretty good.

Although I had no idea what I had in mind by giving back, Pedro seemed to understand. "You could help out the old Jews," he said.

I have to say I was momentarily thrown by his way of putting it. Yes, seeing as it is the Upper West Side and my building has a number of apartments bought at insider prices by people who had been there forever, there was an ample supply of old Jews in residence. But since when did one refer to them that way? Pedro, however, was not a subtle or politically correct sort of guy. He called things as he saw them, and I soon realized that there was no malice in his nomenclature. These people were old; they could barely walk and were very wrinkled. And they were Jews. They spoke to Pedro in heavily accented English, referred to him as "bubbeleh" and "boychik," fed him things like potato kugel, and gave him Hanukkah presents. Being Jews, in other words, was an important part of their identity, and Pedro would have been doing them a disservice had he referred to them in any other way. That I was a "young Jew" did not seem to enter appreciably into Pedro's perception of things. So I let it go.

"How many of them are there?" I asked, "and what do they need?"

Pedro considered the question. "Well," there's the Rosenbaums in 4J. Their aide leaves at 3 and they need someone to work their remote. They like some of the late afternoon reruns." Pedro said he ordinarily had no problem doing this—a fact that went some way toward explaining his heretofore unaccountable absences from the lobby. He liked talking television with the Rosenbaums, he said; they were very jive on the subject, and they always fed him—he was particularly partial to Mrs. Rosenbaum's cheese blintzes. But the building manager had recently instituted stricter rules about his remaining at the front desk, under the assumption that this would help catch the dog with the bladder problem. So far no culprit had been found. Despite the installation of the camera, there had been another incident, so it was decided that any time a dog and owner left the elevator, Pedro was to go in and sniff for evidence.

"There's also Mrs. Schwartz in 7E," he continued in his enumeration of the old Jews who could use my help. "She needs someone to bring up her Meals on Wheels and talk politics. She's very opinionated, so you have to watch your step with her. Then, there's Mr. Brodsky in 11J. But you probably wouldn't want to deal with him."

"Why not?" I asked.

"He's difficult," said Pedro. "I can handle him, but you'd have a hard time."

His dismissive manner was a challenge. "I'll have you know that I grew up with a mother who could compete in mental torture with anyone," I declared proudly, "so I can hold my own with difficult people, thank you."

"Have it your way," shrugged Pedro. "He likes to have someone to talk to after dinner. But he's got a *pisk* on him" (Pedro had picked up some Yiddishisms from the old Jews). "Just don't say I didn't warn you."

THE NEXT DAY, I embarked on my new mission with a visit to the Rosenbaums. When I arrived at their apartment, they were fiddling with the remote, trying to find *Curb Your Enthusiasm*. I checked the paper and told them it wouldn't be on until 5, but they had me sit down and talk a while. Mrs. Rosenbaum had just made a brisket and proceeded to feed me some, even though it was the middle of the afternoon.

"Where's Pedro?" asked Mr. Rosenbaum. He looked at me accusingly, as if he suspected me of murdering Pedro to take his place.

"He has to stay at the front desk," I explained. "I volunteered to help out instead."

"We like Pedro," said Mr. Rosenbaum. "He's a good boychik."

"He loves my blintzes," said Mrs. Rosenbaum.

"I love blintzes," I said.

"My blintzes aren't like other blintzes," said Mrs. Rosenbaum doubtfully.

"Then I'd probably like them even better," I said.

This appeared to assuage her.

"Who are you?" asked Mr. Rosenbaum, still suspicious.

"I'm Suzanne Davis in 8A," I said. "I work at home. That's why I can help you out."

"Hmm," said Mrs. Rosenbaum. "Are you married?"

"No," I sighed regretfully. "I haven't found anyone yet"— I had lately taken to putting my cards on the table upon the advice of Dr. Chitturi, who told me that you need to tell people that you need help; otherwise, how can they know to help you?

Mr. Rosenbaum turned to his wife: "What about your cousin Jacob for her? He lost his wife."

"He's seventy," said Mrs. Rosenbaum. "She's younger."

"So?"

"So she's too young for Jacob."

"Only if she's picky. Are you picky?" he asked me.

"Not really," I said. "But seventy is a little old."

"Then you're picky." He paused. "How about that nephew of yours?"

"Maurice? He's gay," said Mrs. Rosenbaum.

"He is? How do you know?"

"It's obvious."

"What about that nice young man with the dog down the hall? The one who looks like James Bond who moved here from Chicago?"

"He's gay, too," said Mrs. Rosenbaum.

I had to hand it to Mrs. Rosenbaum who, at eighty-five, seemed to have a lot more on the ball in this area than I did.

"She's right," I verified.

"If you're going to be picky, you'll never find anyone," said Mr. Rosenbaum.

They turned on the TV, and I showed them how to use the remote, though it turned out they already knew. They'd been feigning ignorance in order to get Pedro to come up and talk television with them.

"He's the only person we know who watched *The Wire*," said Mrs. Rosenbaum. "Excellent show. Very realistic."

I admitted that I didn't know it. They also liked *Oz* and *Lost*, neither of which I had seen.

"No wonder you can't find a husband," said Mr. Rosenbaum.

"Let me give you a little hint," said Mrs. Rosenbaum. "You probably watch *The Bachelor* and *American Idol*. Only the gay men watch those shows, so unless you want to marry a gay man I suggest you start watching something different."

"I watch *House*," I offered.

"No," Mrs. Rosenbaum shook her head.

"Well, what then?" I asked.

She considered this. "*24* might be good to start with. But it's off the air now."

"*24*," agreed Mr. Rosenbaum. "You didn't have to know anything to follow it; you could catch on right away. But since it's not on, you lost your chance. Jacob likes *24*."

"Enough with Jacob," tsked Mrs. Rosenbaum. "The police dramas are OK, too. Any *CSI*, for example; they're on all the time, so you can see one in a pinch whenever you want."

After the brisket, she served me a few boiled potatoes and carrots, followed by one of her unconventional blintzes, wrapping a few for Pedro, with sour cream the way he liked. "Take my advice and watch *CSI*," she counseled. "You'll have something to talk to the not-gay men about."

As far as dating advice goes, I have to say, I've had worse.

AFTER I GAVE Pedro the blintzes, I brought the Meals on Wheels delivery up to Mrs. Schwartz in 7E.

"Where's Pedro?" she asked suspiciously. "He always brings up my Meals on Wheels."

I explained about the stench of dog urine in the elevator.

She waved her hand: "What's a little pee in the elevator when the world is going to pot?" She pointed to the *New York Times* that lay in disarray on her coffee table. It had clearly been thoroughly perused. "We ought to be marching in the streets. I would if I didn't have a walker."

"What would you march for?" I asked.

"What would I march for? For the overthrow of the government, that's what," she said. She had opened her Meals on Wheels and was peering at it distastefully. "Always an overdone baked potato. But I can't be choosy since I'm on the dole."

I wasn't sure what to say to this, and we were silent a moment; then she asked whether Pedro had gone on strike.

I explained again about the dog problem in the elevator.

"I told him he should go on strike," said Mrs. Schwartz, ignoring what I had said. "They pay him well, but he should do it on principle. Help bring the capitalist machine to its knees." She blinked at me over her bifocals as though registering my presence for the first time. "What do you think, Missy?"

I straightened a bit, sensing that this was not the most respectful mode of address and that maybe I should be offended. "My name is Suzanne," I said, "and I don't know about going on strike."

She gave me a scornful look, then peered at me more closely for a moment. "I think you're my niece," she finally said.

I said I wasn't.

"Well, I think you are," said Mrs. Schwartz, who was obviously used to opposing established opinion. "How's Brenda?"

"Who's Brenda?"

"Your mother."

I said that my mother's name wasn't Brenda.

"How would you know? You don't even know what you think about going on strike."

I said I should at least know the name of my own mother.

"You'd be surprised what most people don't know," said Mrs. Schwartz. "Now read me what those nudniks at the *Times* have to say today." She gestured to the crumpled paper on the coffee table. I found the front page and prepared to read her the headlines.

"Not that," cried Mrs. Schwartz. "I read that propaganda already. The editorial page. That's how you know what the liberal elite are thinking so you can make sure not to think it."

I was struck by her reasoning here. "Are you a Communist?" I asked.

"A Communist," she waved her hand contemptuously. "Of course I'm not a Communist. What do you take me for? I'm an anarchist."

Clearly, Mrs. Schwartz had a more subtle understanding of political movements than I would ever have, so I changed the subject. "What did your husband do?" I asked, hoping to steer her to a more personal and possibly less antagonistic line of discussion.

"He was a presser in the garment district. Worked all his life and what did he get for it?"

"What?"

"Nothing. He's dead."

There followed an indictment of the retail industry that had killed her husband. As I edged out the door, she was railing against the sweatshops in Brazil, where "the tentacles of capitalism were squeezing the life blood out of the third-world proletariat."

"SHE SEEMS ANGRY," I told Pedro after I had fled the tirades of Mrs. Schwartz.

"She's feisty," agreed Pedro.

Feisty did not seem the right word for Mrs. Schwartz's vituperative fury against the social order. "She's an anarchist," I said. "I wonder if she makes bombs in her kitchen."

"She can't get around too well anymore," said Pedro, sounding sorry that Mrs. Schwartz's bomb-making days were behind her. "Mostly, she's just venting because she's depressed. She misses Mort."

Mort, I presumed, was her husband, the dead garment worker.

"You better go up to Brodsky now," said Pedro, "while you still have the energy. Besides, if you come late, he'll only be worse, and he's not easy to begin with."

I'd pretty much had my fill of old Jews by this point—with the result, I have to say, that my respect for Pedro had increased considerably—but I wasn't going to back down on Brodsky after having boasted of my acumen with difficult people. So I went up to 11J and knocked on Saul Brodsky's door.

"Who are you?" asked Brodsky, opening the door a crack and peering at me suspiciously. One thing I'd come to see was that old Jews liked to get to the existential heart of things as quickly as possible.

"I'm Suzanne," I explained. "I'm filling in for Pedro today. He has to watch the elevator to make sure that dogs don't urinate in it."

He opened the door and motioned unenthusiastically for me to come in. He was very old and disheveled, wearing a tattered bathrobe and socks.

"How do they know it's dogs pissing in the elevator? Could be me," said Brodsky, shuffling ahead of me into the living room and throwing a pile of papers onto the floor so I could sit down on the worn sofa.

It was indeed a thought. His apartment was a mess and didn't smell very good either. The altruism that had shown itself in my decision to visit the old Jews to begin with flickered back into life, and I asked if he'd like to have someone (by which I suppose I meant me) come in and help him straighten up.

"No," said Brodsky. "I like it this way. Are your boobs real?"

"Please," I said. "I dropped in to chat, but not about that."

"There you go," said Brodsky. "If you came to do me a favor, then you should chat about what I want to chat about. Otherwise, good riddance to you."

I admitted he had a point.

"So the boobs," he nodded. "Are they real?"

"Yes," I said. "I'm glad you like them."

"I didn't say I liked them. From what I can tell from the TV, everyone gets them done nowadays, so even the not-so-good ones might not be real."

"Thank you for that," I said.

"I didn't say I didn't like them."

"I don't really care what you think," I said, though of course I did. I cared what everybody thought, even a slovenly octogenarian like Brodsky, which (according to Dr. Chitturi) was a large part of my problem.

"So do you have a boyfriend?"

"No," I replied, trying to sound nonchalant. "I'm afraid I'm still single."

"Hmm," said Brodsky appraisingly. "You're not a bad-looking girl, but you're not my type."

"Excuse me," I said. "I'll have Pedro send up another model."

"I don't like sarcastic women," Brodsky countered. "Besides, I've had enough wives. I don't have it in me to handle another."

"How many wives have you had?"

"Three. Four if you count the last one. But I wouldn't marry you. Your boobs aren't big enough. And you're sarcastic."

I have to say that Brodsky was beginning to depress me. I hadn't realized that as part of my social work I would have to be rejected by an eighty-seven-year-old man.

"I could give you a try in the sack if you promise to keep your mouth shut and do most of the work. But I won't marry you."

I must have looked hurt because he continued, "I know someone who might like you, though. My nephew—but he might be gay."

CHAPTER

9

I HAVE TO ADMIT that the old Jews, though not polite, were colorful, so by the end of the week, I had gotten to a point where I enjoyed visiting them, in a masochistic sort of way. One day, however, when I stopped by the front desk to pick up Mrs. Schwartz's Meals on Wheels, Pedro informed me that, though I was free to continue the visits on my own account, I was no longer obliged to do so as his replacement. The management had caught the guilty dog or, given that dogs really can't be blamed for this sort of thing, the guilty dog owners. It was one of the bichons in the bandanna who, it seems, had a weak bladder and would dribble. Pedro had caught a whiff after the couple exited the elevator at 7 one evening when I was upstairs having Brodsky reject me.

There seemed to me to be a lesson in this discovery, insofar as the Wetsons, as the couple was aptly named, had seemed so above the fray at the Doggie Meet and Greet. The seemingly most innocent often happen to be the guiltiest—or, as Eleanor likes to say, you can't trust a goddamn soul. This is a dictum she has embraced religiously ever since her seemingly listless and ineffectual husband was discovered to be engaged in high-level financial chicanery while frequenting expensive call girls on the side. Ronnie had never seemed to be very smart, which must have been his cover, and a very shrewd one at that. It brought to mind the "appearance versus reality" essays I had written in my college Shakespeare class. We'd all written them, though no one, as far as I knew, ever registered the fact that they might have some connection to the way things happened in actual life. But Ronnie was right out of one of those papers. He had duped hundreds of people by appearing to be a boring, garden-variety dunce. Unlike many of the men I had dated, whose bad character was of a more subtle variety and whose infidelities could not be simply condemned (and might, in fact, be blamed on me), Eleanor's ex was a wolf in lamb's clothing—underneath his ineffectual facade he was a scoundrel, pure and simple. There was real catharsis in that.

The Wetsons offered a similar if not quite as far-reaching dramatic revelation. They had presented themselves as model citizens, occupying the doggie elite of the building. Now that they had fallen from their pedestal, they would have to slink around with their tails between their legs, so to speak. I noted that the bandannas, the emblems of their complacency, disappeared once they were unmasked. I also learned from Philip and his partner Kurt (who were now my devoted friends) that the Wetsons had ceased frequenting Riverside Park and been sighted in Central Park, a real schlep and generally considered an inconvenient and déclassé dog area by the experts in our building. Justice, at least of a dog-centric variety, had been served.

CHAPTER

10

I'D BEEN MEETING Pauline for lunch on a weekly basis for a few months now, and she'd been trying to get me to start coming to book club again, explaining that if I was interested in getting Derek back, it was just a matter of time. The reconciliation with Bathsheba was not going well. They had had a fight during the discussion of sleeplessness in *One Hundred Years of Solitude*, when Bathsheba had begun complaining that Derek snored right through the kids' crying and that it was the old story all over again. He had lashed back: "It's never enough for you. You're insatiable. I improve and you raise the bar."

"They're thinking of marriage counseling," said Pauline, "but it's my opinion that Bathsheba is very demanding and he won't be able to meet her standards. I know he'd love to get back with you again, if you're really interested." She was obviously trying to gauge whether my standards were lower than Bathsheba's, which wouldn't say much for me.

I therefore proceeded to spell things out: I had no interest in Derek anymore and, indeed, had never had much interest in him to begin with.

"Thank goodness," said Pauline, as though she could now finally be frank and also view me with more respect. "He really is a monumental asshole," she observed.

I have to say that I appreciated Pauline's sensitivity here. She had kept this uninflected assessment of Derek to herself until she knew where I stood. This is the sign of good manners, I explained to Eleanor, who has a habit of blurting out her opinion of people with whom I have not yet become disillusioned, thereby creating awkwardness between us until I come around to her view. Eleanor insists that it's the role of a friend to speak the truth no matter what, and that she would have appreciated it if I had been franker with her about Ronnie, who everyone except her seemed to realize was worthless, though without guessing he was also a gigantic sociopath; if I had spoken out, maybe she would have thought twice.

I could see her point, but I still liked Pauline's tact, which might also be attributed to the fact that she hadn't known me since the fourth grade and wasn't familiar with my abysmal record with men.

"There's always Stephen," Pauline noted now.

I remembered the colloquy I'd had with Stephen during the Doggie Meet and Greet, and how he had seemed less wispy than I originally thought.

"He's the math teacher I had in mind to begin with," clarified Pauline. "He's smart, though he may be too serious for you."

I don't know if this was meant to incite me to prove her wrong or just a simple statement of fact. That I was frivolous and not very smart was not an illogical deduction based on my fling with Derek and my misunderstanding about Philip.

The latter, I should note, had at least yielded benefits, which is more than I can say for the former. Philip and Kurt had already had me back to dinner twice: once for blackened char and once for mussels in a white wine reduction. Both men were gourmet chefs and deep into fish. The tilapia and sun-dried tomatoes should have been a giveaway during that initial conversation, but then lots of things should have been a giveaway. We had all laughed uproariously about my dimwittedness as we enjoyed these subsequent expertly prepared dinners.

"It's not entirely your fault," Kurt had said, ladling out the mussels. "Philip has that effect on women, and he's so sweet that he doesn't realize it."

This was said with that mixture of flattery and facetiousness that somehow only a gay man can carry off, which left me wondering whether Philip was actually not so sweet and had realized exactly what he was doing: leading unsuspecting women like myself on to what, in reality TV parlance, would be called "the great reveal." This was in keeping with Eleanor's dictum not to trust anyone, and it had the further advantage of allowing me not to label myself a complete moron. When I mentioned this to Philip and Kurt, they only laughed harder and glanced flirtatiously at each other, which I suppose could be taken to support my theory.

But it was all water under the bridge now, and they had become very interested in my love life and promised to keep a lookout for me, though they admitted they didn't really know any eligible men. Most of their friends were either gay or women like me. Hanging out with them was like being in San Francisco without the hills.

CHAPTER

11

EXCEPT FOR PAULINE, I hadn't seen the playground women for a long time. But one day I got a call from Iris, mother of the pugnacious Daniel. She was sobbing, saying that I was the only one she had to turn to, which struck me as a reason in itself to be upset.

It turns out that Daniel had hit the in-vitro-generated Matthew with an action figure in a blow that had come very close to the eye. Karen had declared this to be the last straw and had spearheaded a campaign to have Daniel banished from the playground. It was true, Iris admitted, that Daniel was an energetic, high-spirited boy with an emergent case of ADHD, but he meant no harm, anyone could see that, and Matthew was a fearful, overprotected child whose mother went berserk over every little scratch and had singled out Daniel as the scapegoat for her anxiety.

Yet, Iris concluded tearfully, though all this was patently obvious to everyone, the other mothers had not come to her defense. Karen had special status as a result of her more advanced age and her long and expensive in-vitro ordeal. No one felt inclined to challenge her. Iris, by contrast, was an ordinary mother. She had no claim to prestige and thus no following, which is why she had turned to me as an unallied individual with a connection, albeit a tenuous one, to the activity of the playground.

"Even though you pretend to be cynical, everyone knows you have a heart of gold," Iris noted as an addendum to why she had contacted me. "I noticed how you played so well with your boyfriend's kids."

"Ex-boyfriend," I corrected, feeling a momentary pang. The fact is that though I didn't miss Derek, I did miss his boys and had even contemplated asking him to drop them off for a play date—if I hadn't worried that it would sound too pathetic.

Iris's observation regarding my heart of gold (something that, presumably, the other playground mothers were privy to as well) took me aback. I hadn't realized that anyone had been paying close enough attention to come up with such a layered assessment of my personality. Dr. Chitturi always said that my sarcasm was a defense, and that I'm actually a very sensitive person, deeply desirous of pleasing and doing what's right. But Dr. Chitturi is my therapist, for God's sake; I pay her to put a good spin on me. But for Iris and her friends, engrossed in the vicissitudes of toilet training and pre-school enrichment, to arrive at such a conclusion was surprising. Perhaps they were all more perceptive than I'd given them credit for. Perhaps Iris, at least, had developed a knack for character analysis from having to decipher Daniel's violent nonverbal behavior. Or perhaps she was just trying to butter me up so that I would do her bidding.

"Won't you come and help me talk to them?" Iris concluded plaintively. "The other mothers have so much respect for you, as a person and a writer."

She was now scraping the bottom of the barrel, but it didn't matter; I was hooked. I agreed to help out, either because I have a heart of gold or because I was a sucker for flattery—you decide.

CHAPTER

12

W<small>HEN WE ARRIVED</small> at the playground the next morning, most of the mothers had already assembled at the picnic table behind the swing set. As we approached, Karen was in the process of holding forth on the need to protect their children from bullies like Daniel.

Karen had initially struck me as a nondescript, shy sort of person. Both on the playground and at book club she had been soft-spoken and reticent. But the injury to Matthew had activated some latent but powerful part of her being, and she now took a strident, rabble-rousing stance. It was a case, in another register, of what I had observed with the seemingly-humdrum-turned-extravagantly-predatory Ronnie: still waters run deep.

The other mothers were not sure how to react to Karen's furious eruption, and were glancing nervously at each other as Iris and I walked toward them with the guilty Daniel in tow.

As we neared the group, Karen stepped forward to block our approach. "I'm afraid Daniel is not welcome to join the other children," she announced.

The other mothers drew together expectantly. There was excitement in the air as everyone looked forward to a fight that they would have the luxury of not having a stake in.

"I beg your pardon?" said Iris.

"Daniel has shown himself to be a violent and dangerous child, and we cannot risk having our children exposed to him," Karen continued.

Daniel, meanwhile, understanding vaguely that they were speaking about him and that it was not flattering, began to whimper.

Karen spelled it out: "We are asking your son to leave."

The other mothers looked slightly sheepish in being affiliated with this inflexible opposition, but did not protest. Karen had an air of barely contained hysteria, and no one wanted to risk having so much unpredictable emotion turned in their direction.

"I live in this building, and I will not have my child barred from my own playground," said Iris.

"This playground is a community space, and your child is a menace," Karen retorted.

Daniel's whimpering had now escalated to outright bawling, causing the other mothers to look at each other in consternation. A child who could cry couldn't be all bad, and the suspicion began to emerge that Karen might be going too far. It may have occurred to them that if Daniel was a bully, Karen was one too, and she was forty-five years old.

Feeling the tide turn, it struck me that this might be a good time to intercede.

"May I say a word?" I broke in tentatively.

"What do you want?" snapped Karen, turning on me angrily. "You don't belong here. You don't even have a child."

This was a low blow for which I was not prepared. Tears welled up in my eyes, a response that, as it turned out, worked to my benefit. The other mothers noticed and grew quiet. It was sad enough that I didn't have a child of my own, but rubbing it in was simply going too far. I could see that Karen had lost a good deal of leverage in making both Daniel and me cry in the course of a few minutes.

But in the temporary lull of that moment I also had a revelation. The play group had appealed to me in one respect, if in nothing else—it had seemed to promote kindness as a value. Kindness was something in short supply in this world, and I had, if only unconsciously, warmed to the notion that these mothers, despite their inane preoccupations, had created a utopia based on this value. Daniel's ostracism from the group contradicted this idea, and it was this violation, I realized, that bothered me. If mothers and their kids couldn't be kind to each other, who the hell could? There would be no solving the crisis in the Middle East, for one thing, if this presumably most benign group on earth couldn't figure out how to get along.

At the same time, I must concede that I also understood Karen's response. Who was I to meddle in these women's business? What did I know about child-rearing? To my surprise, however, I no sooner raised these questions in my own mind than I answered them reflexively out loud, stepping forward to address Karen and the other mothers with uncharacteristic forcefulness: "It is precisely because I *don't* have a child of my own that I feel entitled to address you all," I said, wiping away the tears that I pretended had made it down my cheeks (a few of which actually had). "As someone who isn't blessed as you are, I feel obliged to remind you of the sacred trust that accompanies your good fortune." I now assumed some of the spirited verbosity of a civil rights preacher: "You must not, tempting though it is, retreat into selfish complacency, caring only for your own child," I said, looking severely at Karen. "You should, instead, see your-selves as the mothers of all"—I made a sweeping motion at the toddlers who had begun rifling through the Vera Bradley quilted bags in search of juice boxes and fruit snacks—"and help make a better, more equitable world, where all children are nurtured and accepted. You have it in your power to pro-duce a better world, where the lion will lie down with the lamb"—I motioned to Daniel, the lion, and Matthew, the lamb. "This challenge is bestowed on you as a sacred trust, and I call on you, from the bottom of my heart, to meet it."

The mothers were staring at me, wondering for a second what to make of my words—which most people would have put down to the ravings of a lunatic. But, let's face it, when it comes to New York mothers, there's no amount of mean-ing that you can impose on their role that they won't accept. Savior of the western world? Sure. Model for peace and pros-perity? They could buy that. The whole "sacred trust" thing fit in perfectly with their need to justify having quit that job in high finance, dropped out of med school, thumbed their nose at the fellowship opportunity at the London School of Economics, in order to spend their days slicing apples and watching *SpongeBob SquarePants*.

There was a murmur of approval from the mothers, and after some whispering and affectionate pushing, Iris and Karen actually hugged. There was applause. Everyone began to cry. The mothers surged forward to embrace the fright-ened Daniel. Matthew was paraded up and thrust into Dan-iel's arms. The whole thing, really, was pretty dramatic, and had you told me that I had it in me to negotiate such a resolu-tion, I wouldn't have believed you.

AND SO IT ALL was happily resolved: Daniel would be worked over by the mothers and taught to be less aggressive, while

Matthew would be encouraged to stand up for himself and not depend so much on maternal protection. This seemed like an acceptable compromise for all concerned, and Karen was able to relax and discuss the literature of risk relating to Matthew's next vaccine, which, as it turned out, was really what was worrying her anyway.

After it was over, Pauline came up to me. "I have to congratulate you," she said. "I should have done it. I really shirked my duty there. But Daniel threw sand in Rose's face last week, and I felt I couldn't afford to antagonize Karen, given what she went through. But you were right, of course. We lose sight of the larger picture, spending all our time around our own children. You were fabulous with that stuff about moral responsibility and being a model for world peace. I mean, that was high-level negotiation rhetoric. I'm telling you, you have a gift."

Pauline paused at this juncture to consider her own words. During her years as a mover and shaker in the work-place, she had been particularly adept in the area of human resources, and the prospect of putting me to use seemed to strike her forcibly. "They could certainly use you in the mayor's office, with the sanitation workers," she noted. "They're always threatening to strike; it's a real problem. But bad as they are, they're not half as hard to manage as Karen. You could be a definite asset to the city if you used your skills with them. I'll speak to Roger about it, if you're interested."

CHAPTER

13

THE PROSPECT OF a new job as a sanitation-worker negotiator, seductive though it might be, flew out of my mind when I meandered into the I-ACE headquarters the next morning.

I may have mentioned that I was not obliged to report regularly to my site of employment. No one at I-ACE cared where I did my work so long as a certain number of press releases and conference abstracts were put on file so that the organization could say that it was engaged in "public outreach," written into its charter as one of its myriad of useless functions. The fact is, my employers didn't really expect people outside their own group of specialized nerds to care about air conditioning, and so they didn't really expect my efforts to amount to much. This made my job very easy, low expectations being the friend of the lackadaisical worker.

That said, the guys in the office were always happy to see me when I chose to make an appearance. As I may also have noted, I-ACE members are not a prepossessing bunch in general, and those employed by the organization are, if possible, even less so.

The in-house workers in question consisted of three individuals with jobs so technical that, given my non-technical background in technical writing, I couldn't make head or tail of them. I think they were involved with something to do with establishing, testing, and revising standards for the industry, but what those standards consisted of, I couldn't say, and what it was they did all day, since they, unlike me, were, for reasons of necessity or lack of imagination, actually there in the office, I couldn't say either.

Two of the three, Walt and Dave, were in their fifties and looked as if they had spent their lives in a cave, which, in a manner of speaking, they had—I-ACE headquarters being a cramped space which, ironically enough, is poorly ventilated. The guys were always complaining about this fact but never managing to rectify it (a bad sign, as I saw it, from a public relations standpoint, but, since I was rarely at the office, not an issue I was inclined to make a fuss over).

Walt, the senior of the two, was extremely obese and wore pants that held his massive girth in an uneven sling. He had a large droopy face and wore small dirty eyeglasses that he was always wiping with a dirty handkerchief plucked from some mysterious part of his lumpy anatomy. It was hard to look at Walt straight on, which meant that I tended to focus more on the other two. Dave was not fat, I'm happy to say, but he also had an unhealthy demeanor: a sallow complexion and thin, graying hair that he combed across his head like strips of undercooked bacon. Dave was a smoker and was always nervously touching his breast pocket, where he kept his cigarettes, as though promising himself that if he only held on and did a little more of whatever he was doing, he would allow himself to go outside and stand in the garbage-strewn alley behind the I-ACE headquarters and suck on a cigarette.

The third employee, Roy, was, comparatively speaking, the most attractive and couth of the three. This, however, was not saying much. Roy was about forty years old and not overweight or pasty, since he did not overeat or smoke. On the contrary, his habits were extremely careful and pre-scribed. He usually brought a whole-grain sandwich to work and would leave the office for an hour or so during the day to take a long walk. These commendable habits were overshad-owed, however, by the fact that he seemed set on some sort of timer and did everything by rote. Roy, as it turned out, lived with his mother in Queens and continued to be as obe-dient at forty as he had been at four. Both Walter and Dave were vaguely married—the idea that women were attached to these men strained the imagination but was nonethe-less true, given the fact that they both had wedding bands embedded in the flesh of their left ring fingers. Roy had clearly never gone on a date, much less contemplated matri-mony. He had fresh pink cheeks that had never seen a razor and large rheumy eyes that always looked as if they were gaz-ing out at life for the first time and not making much sense of what they saw.

At my most desperate moments, I would sometimes con-sider Roy as a romantic prospect. I would imagine him blos-soming, under my tutelage, into a fascinating consort, capa-ble of surprising sexual antics. This scenario was one that I periodically entertained at 2 or 3 A.M., after being seduced and then rejected by one of those charming, predatory types who are the opposite of Roy. But whenever I visited I-ACE headquarters and saw Roy in the flesh, the scenario would evaporate. There was just no way that Roy's emphatically neutered person could be jump-started for my purposes. To make Roy into a viable partner would be the equivalent of making a rubber duck into a living creature with feathers.

Visiting I-ACE was therefore not something I particularly relished, but when I did do it I have to say I made an effort. I felt I was doing a good deed—like one of those starlets visiting the troops: they don't want to get too close, but for the moment on the stage, with all that whistling and applause, there's bound to be a rush. Thus it was that when I would traipse into I-ACE headquarters, all work would come to a halt and the three guys would turn their unprepossessing faces in my direction expectantly. Walt would turn down his radio—he listened to Golden Oldies—and the others would look up from their treatises and proceedings and allow me to regale them with tales from the outside world.

I felt I could really say almost anything to these guys; they took it as my style, and they followed the saga of my life the way people follow a soap opera. They knew about my annoying mother, and my series of hopeless relationships, including my misunderstanding with Wordsworth and Philip. Usually, I came in with a story prepared for them, but sometimes I took requests, which keyed me in to their particular interests. Walt and Dave liked to hear about my miserable love life, Roy about my abusive mother—which I suppose says something about their particular repressions.

Occasionally, when I entered the squalid headquarters office, some of the members of the organization, air-conditioning engineers from "out in the field," so to speak, would be there to discuss some piece of air-conditioning arcana or confer over a paper they planned to deliver at the I-ACE convention held annually in Parsippany, New Jersey (due to the prohibitive cost of hotels in Manhattan). These visitors, usually members from Delaware or New Jersey with a little vacation time on their hands, were all variations of Walt, Dave, or Roy. Evidently air-conditioning engineers came in these three varieties, like standard flavors of ice cream: large and soiled, thin and stained, or plain asexual—three brands that, as far as I could see, left very little room to maneuver for someone with her biological clock ticking.

But on this particular visit, I was in for a surprise. A different sort of person was lounging near the cluttered desk behind which Walt's massive girth was spread, and I could see at a glance that he did not fit into the three kinds of men that generally make up the I-ACE selection.

This man was a wiry specimen, slim and well dressed in what I immediately perceived to be a European style. One can tell a European man by the way his clothes fit—they hug his body rather than draping loosely in the American manner. European men also wear shoes molded to the foot like a modified ballet slipper, not the sort of clodhoppers that reflect the bull-in-a-china-shop style of the American man in almost any situation. The European weaves and insinuates, the American clomps and pushes—there you have it in a nutshell. This man was European, and I soon learned his name was Yves Guiset, a genuine Frenchman, come all the way from France to confer about a new air-conditioning technology that he wanted to receive the I-ACE seal of approval.

Yves's innovation, as I soon learned over aperitifs at the Carlyle, where he whisked me off almost as soon as he saw me, was a new system calibrated to prevent the sort of frigid air conditioning that had become the norm in American office buildings.

"With my system," said Yves, leaning toward me seductively, "you will no longer have to wear a sweater to work in the summertime. You will be able to wear your pretty little summer dresses and your pretty, very small blouses, without fear of freezing."

I have to say that I was taken by Yves's innovation quite as much as I was taken with Yves. I am one of those women who, during the summer months, suffer from excessive air conditioning the way others suffer from hay fever. I carry large handbags exclusively for the purpose of lugging sweaters and scarves to protect myself against air conditioning. I have had dates in fancy restaurants ruined by being seated under the air-conditioning vent; a desire to escape the frigid blast has obscured the poor man's possibly sterling qualities. Older women have told me that in time air conditioning will be my friend, but currently—and I suppose until my biological clock clicks to its appointed end—I consider air conditioning my enemy. This is all the more paradoxical since my work is with those responsible for it. Now here was a Frenchman, dressed in a body-hugging suit and supple loafers, with a small pointed face and piercing dark eyes, offering to solve my air-conditioning problem while plying me with aperitifs at the Carlyle Hotel. How could I not go to bed with him?

But I am getting ahead of myself. Yves had prepared a paper to be delivered at the I-ACE annual convention in March. His hope, and the reason for his advance trip to New York, was to get his innovation approved by various U.S. regulatory groups and to build, as he put it in his delightfully broken English, "a swelling ground" of support for it among the general populace. His notion seemed to be that a great deal of enthusiasm was likely to accrue to the idea of a non-frigid air-conditioning system if only he could get the word out in the proper places. My job, he seemed to feel, was crucial in this respect. He was keen to have me edit his paper so that it would read more smoothly for industry dissemination, and also, more importantly, to have me distill its message into a press release for the various news outlets that he was sure were clamoring for it. Given that he was adorable, plying me with drinks and making goo-goo eyes at me all over the city, I wasn't about to disabuse him of his inflated idea of my usefulness in effecting these ends.

For the next five days, therefore, I showed Yves the sights of New York, stopping for aperitifs and repasts of various sorts, talking air conditioning (as far as I was capable), and slowly moving toward the inevitable culmination of it all, i.e., a tumultuous night of love. How I managed to put this event off for almost a week is beyond me. I think, despite his protestations, that Yves was helpful in this regard. He was scheduled to return to France in ten days, and we all know that the French are experts at foreplay.

I wrote a draft or two of a press release on the subject of his "non-frigid air-conditioning system" (as he liked to refer to it) that we pored over, our bodies touching and giving me a frisson of anticipation, as I crossed out and added to the fact sheet on how the new system would work.

By the fifth day, when we appeared to be getting along swimmingly, my fantasies about life in France—Yves was from the south not far from the Côte d'Azur—had taken on a lush and vibrant hue. It seemed that he came from a family of some wealth. His parents lived in a château—a small one, he protested, and a bit run down, but very *sympa* (which, I learned, means "nice" in French slang). "You will like it," he said enticingly. When a Frenchman says that you will like his château, how can you not let your fantasies a little bit loose? I began to imagine what it would be like to move to the South of France, live in a château, albeit a small one, and learn to prepare dishes like coq au vin and sole meunière for Yves and his friends.

Still, I'm not a complete idiot; I did ask him some questions. I said, "Yves—have you been married?"

He waved his hand. "Married, *bien sûr*. But that was a long time ago. French women are very disdainful, very cold—unlike American women."

What, pray tell, would you have made of that? That he was divorced from a cold and disdainful French woman and looking for a warm and spontaneous American woman to take her place in the château? Precisely what I made of it. And like me, you would have been wrong.

By the fifth day, as I said, my resistance was so low that even a vague hint that I might perhaps want to accompany him back to his hotel was met with unabashed enthusiasm. I think, retrospectively, that Yves would have preferred to have me hold out until the last day of his visit, but by now I had become what he considered a typical American woman: lacking in all calculation and very, very hot to roll around in the sack with him.

It turned out that he was staying in a boutique hotel frequented by French people. There are many such ethnically niched hotels in New York, and the French are particularly keen to stay in hotels run and frequented by their own nationality. In a hotel of this sort they can continue to lord it over Americans, even in America. Because all the employees in Yves's hotel were French, he spoke to them in his native language, making me feel, when I accompanied him to the front desk, like a foreigner and a bit of a tramp. The young woman with well-applied makeup behind the desk eyed me contemptuously, gave Yves his key, and, I could swear, winked at him as we went upstairs.

I will admit that Yves was an attentive and excellent lover. This, too, could have been predicted. Frenchmen, unlike Americans, take their time, and Yves's delectation of my body was something akin to the way I eat a very good pastry—slowly, savoring it, and when it's done, vaguely regretting having eaten it.

The regret part was not evident to me right away. Indeed, I am so used to having American men fall into a profound slumber after making love that Yves's relative alertness struck me as a tribute to my charms. Also impressive was the fact that he had ordered a post-coital meal. The young woman with the well-applied makeup knocked and, not waiting for a reply, entered (giving me barely time to pull the covers up over my recently ravished nakedness). She thumped the tray down on the night table and began chattering to Yves in rapid French, her eyes darting at me with contemptuous amusement as she did so.

"What did she say?" I asked after she'd gone.

"Oh nothing," said Yves. "She just wanted to know what I wanted for breakfast tomorrow."

This seemed to me precisely what she had not said, but I let it go.

We continued to loll in bed, sipping on the cheap champagne that the girl at the desk had brought up. I noted that Yves had his eye on the clock.

I asked him what it was he was waiting for.

"A phone call from France," he said. "There it is." The phone indeed was ringing, and Yves picked it up and began speaking in animated French. The conversation, lively and full of laughter, went on for about fifteen minutes—which I have to say I found a bit rude, since there I was buck naked in bed, having finally succumbed to this man's seductive entreaty after five days of intensive courtship.

Toward the end of the phone call, Yves spoke rapidly in a low and ardent voice of the sort that I recalled he had used on me only that afternoon. He ended by making kissing sounds into the phone.

Needless to say, I was curious and alarmed. I had imagined that our lovemaking was the prelude to something serious, but here he was smacking his lips and whispering seductively to someone else, even as I lay naked beside him.

"Who was that?" I asked after he hung up.

"Oh," said Yves, "that was my wife."

"Your wife? You said you were divorced."

"I never said that," he protested. "I have been married to Marie-Thérèse for ten years. We have two children, Gilles and Lorraine."

"I see," I said. "I thought the woman you married was disdainful and cold."

"She is," shrugged Yves. "I like that about her."

This was a wake-up call. A cultural rift seemed to open up as we spoke. Perhaps the French liked disdainful and cold; if so, that placed my spontaneity and warmth in an entirely different light.

Yves must have seen the expression on my face because he looked eager to assuage me. "But I very much like you," he said. "You are very American. I hope to see you when I come back for the annual meeting. We will work on a new press release and have many nice evenings together."

By now I had begun to hurriedly get dressed. The sooner I got myself out of Yves's hotel room the better, I thought, for my fragile psyche.

"What's wrong?" he asked. He seemed genuinely confused by my behavior.

"You didn't tell me about Gilles and Lorraine," I said.

"Why should I tell you? It's boring to hear about other people's children."

"Or that you liked the fact that your wife was disdainful and cold."

"But I also like spontaneous and warm," said Yves. To his credit, I think he probably liked both. It was like having a taste for a hamburger and a hot dog; they're not mutually exclusive.

By the time I was dressed and ready to leave, I had calmed down a bit and could acknowledge that Yves, though vaguely duplicitous, was not actually malevolent. He had assumed that I, like him, had my own agenda. He liked women and he liked aperitifs. Sex, too, though that wasn't at the very top of his list. That place was reserved for air-conditioning systems, which were really his first and best love. How could he possibly have imagined that I was fantasizing about living in a chateau, cooking coq au vin, and having little Gilles and Lorraines of my own? I mean, that would have been too pathetic.

CHAPTER

14

Was I eternally fated to make an ass of myself with men? Eleanor, a morbid truth teller, said yes. She'd known me since the fourth grade, and I'd been doing it since then; why would I change? Pauline, with a more positive attitude and a devotion to self-improvement, said no; she saw my romantic disasters, numerous though they might be, as learning experiences that would eventually lead to success.

I liked Pauline's answer better, although I did realize that it had points in common with the way she spoke to Rose when Rose had trouble coloring inside the lines in her coloring book: "Keep trying, sweetie; you'll get there." Still, it was nice to have someone believe in me other than Dr. Chitturi, whom I was paying to believe in me. And so I let Pauline go on and on about the value of making mistakes, how if you're thrown from the horse, it's important to get right back on, and other comforting platitudes.

She also took the opportunity to start nagging me again about coming back to book club. I had put her off on the subject for weeks, book club being what had launched me into my unsavory affair with Derek and thus tainted by that association. But Pauline made the point that it was weak-minded to let Derek define the experience. "Besides, we need you back," she said. "Bathsheba is so smug and pedantic, and she's always picking on Derek. If he weren't such a monumental asshole, I might feel sorry for him. We need you to lift the level of the discussion." This was definitely aimed at stimulating my vanity, which it did, my vanity being easily stimulated.

But what really convinced me to go back to book club were the supplications of Philip and Kurt, who wanted to join. They needed intellectual stimulation, they said, and this would allow them to meet Derek and thereby be in a position to ridicule him for my benefit, as the true friends they were. This too appealed to me.

When I told Pauline about bringing along Philip and Kurt, she was enthusiastic: "It would be great to have them," she said. "We need to break out of our demographic. I've been telling Roger to get some of the black mayoral aides to join, but he says they've already been snapped up by the more multicultural clubs. I'm so glad your gay friends are available."

Thus, when I finally succumbed to Pauline's urging to return to book club, I did so with Philip and Kurt in tow. The meeting was held, as usual, in Pauline's apartment, no one else being in a position, due to lack of space or unmanageable clutter, to serve as host. As soon as I walked in, I noticed Derek sitting next to an imposing-looking woman in expensive hippie-ish garb, a mop of artfully disheveled hair, and an expression of extreme annoyance on her face. This, I surmised, was Bathsheba. Derek had his familiar hangdog look, but seemed to brighten when I entered and immediately shot moon eyes in my direction, which I studiously ignored. How I could have possibly found this man attractive was now beyond me. My wonder at the fact seemed to mark some sort of progress—and I made a note to tell Dr. Chitturi.

As I looked around, I noticed that the cushions that had been used in the past for makeshift seating had disappeared and that chairs had been brought in from the dining room to replace them. As Pauline explained to me later, Bathsheba had objected to the cushions. She did not have to sit on one herself; there was plenty of room for her on the sofa next to Marsha and Herb, but she had decided that Derek looked foolish sitting on a cushion and that he should not do so. This had caused a skirmish, as Derek said he wanted to sit on a cushion and didn't care if he looked foolish, to which she replied that he might not care, but that she did; she was married to him and thus his foolishness reflected on her.

Pauline had recounted this contretemps as evidence of the incipient demise of the relationship. "I'm not against having strong opinions," she noted, "or trying to control your husband's behavior within reason. I insist, for example, that Roger not belch in front of Rose, drink beer from the bottle, or put his feet up on the couch. But you have to pick your battles. If you start worrying about his looking foolish doing this or that, you'll never get to the end of it. Men look foolish practically all the time, especially when you're married to them, and if you can't accept that, you shouldn't bother being married." This is one of the many nuggets of wisdom that Pauline has imparted to me in the course of our friendship.

Nonetheless, Pauline had accommodated Bathsheba in removing the cushions and bringing in the chairs. Derek and Bathsheba were seated on two of these, next to each other but angled so that they were facing in opposite directions. Marsha and Herb were, as usual, sprawled on the couch, while Karen and David were again seated on the low chairs in front of the coffee table. Additional chairs had been set out for Philip, Kurt, and me. I noted that Stephen, the wispy math teacher (who I had recently discovered was not really wispy), was absent. I felt a pang of disappointment, recalling the conversation we had had at the Doggie Meet and Greet when he surprised me by remembering something I'd said at book club months earlier. This had indicated that he was a good listener. And a man who listens well is about as rare as a well-priced New York apartment that doesn't face a brick wall.

"He's taking a hiatus from group," explained Pauline; "he won't say why, but he sends his regrets." She said this and sighed, and I could tell that what she really meant was "you had your chance, and now he's probably met someone else"— which, I admit, immediately raised my opinion of him. According to Dr. Chitturi, this is one of those patterns (i.e., thinking more highly of people when someone else decides they're worthwhile) that I need to work on.

Once we had all assembled, Pauline took a few moments to thank Kurt and Philip for coming and supplying the gay perspective. She didn't say this in so many words, but her reference to "the panache of a new viewpoint" had to be code for the gay perspective.

I thought she would dislodge Marsha and Herb from the sofa in order to give Kurt and Philip the place of honor, but they insisted on taking the chairs next to me. When we were finally settled, we all got out our books—*Daisy Miller*, chosen by Pauline because Henry James is an important writer whom everyone remembers having vaguely disliked reading in college. This, for Pauline, constituted a powerful incentive to read him again.

"Shall we get started?" She clapped her hands in the manner of a first-grade teacher.

"Why are all the women in the books we read named Daisy?" asked Derek, a question that everyone ignored.

"Personally, I can't understand what all the fuss was about in this book," Pauline launched in. "I know Henry James is supposed to be profound, but I couldn't see the point he was going for here."

"Couldn't get into it either," noted Roger. "Very wordy, no action."

"They assigned this story in my freshman English class in college," said Derek, glad to partake of the consensus view. "I couldn't read it then, and I couldn't read it now."

"You can't read anything," Bathsheba observed. "You have the attention span of a flea."

Everyone grew still at this barb, worried but also hoping that an entertaining fight might ensue.

"I happen to be busy with a job, unlike some people," Derek responded after a pause—it was hard to attack Bathsheba in substantive terms; even on short acquaintance, I could see that most of her flaws were of the ineffable pain-in-the-ass sort.

In this instance, moreover, Derek's attack was ill-chosen, given the number of stay-at-home mothers present. Pauline and Karen both looked daggers in his direction, and Bathsheba, knowing she had this powerful phalanx behind her, straightened proudly: "I have a job," she replied righteously. "I am the mother of our children. Indeed, this is more than a job; it is a calling. And yet I still manage to keep my brain alive."

"Just because you read *The New Yorker* doesn't make you an intellectual giant," rejoined Derek.

Heads had been turning back and forth as if at a tennis match in which it was clear in advance who was going to win. It was only a matter of time before Bathsheba would hit a fast low ball to a corner that Derek could not reach.

"You cannot possibly know what I read, since your eyes are glued to the television as soon as you get home. You'd think a grown man would be ashamed to watch those reality shows." This was a low blow—no one likes to be accused of watching reality TV, and I happen to know that Derek has a predilection for *The Bachelor*, having caught him engrossed in it more than once when he thought I was in the shower.

"So what did *you* think of the book, Bathsheba?" Pauline intervened. Although she enjoyed a good fight as much as the rest of us, she also felt obliged to keep book club on track.

"It seemed lightweight," Bathsheba replied, still glaring at Derek. "But then, I prefer *late* James. I happened to recently complete *The Golden Bowl*, which is 900 pages in the Penguin edition, *in between* reading *The New Yorker*."

This seemed to give her the match, and everyone settled back to resume the discussion.

"Having the heroine catch malaria because she stayed out too late in the Roman forum was pretty contrived," noted David. "I didn't buy it."

"Can you really catch malaria that way?" asked Karen worriedly. In her concern for Matthew's well-being, she seemed prepared to cross Rome off her list of future vacation spots.

"I don't think so," Pauline reassured her. "That was the nineteenth century. I'm sure they've solved the mosquito problem by now."

"I don't care what you people say—I loved the book," said Kurt. "Daisy was a free spirit—an unfettered, spontaneous American girl."

"A shooting star," agreed Philip.

"But none too bright," noted Marsha.

"She reminded me of a girl I used to date," said Herb. "Good-hearted but flighty."

"Did she die young?"

"No, she married a contractor in South Jersey."

"What do you think, Suzanne?" asked Pauline, graciously turning to me.

I'd read *Daisy Miller*, along with *The Great Gatsby*, in my American Studies class in college, where the discussion had focused on Kurt's point: Daisy Miller as the quintessential American girl. I personally didn't buy it. After all, *I* am an American girl, and *I* wouldn't go gallivanting off to the Roman forum at night if everyone said I would catch malaria. I hate mosquitoes, and I'd sooner meet someone in a nice hotel bar. I said this to the group, and it was well received as an example of my rapier wit.

But as I was talking I also realized that it wasn't really Daisy Miller who interested me. It was the narrator, who was telling us what happened to Daisy Miller and whose relationship with her never got off the ground. "This guy, Winterbourne, bothers me," I proceeded to announce. "Daisy wanted him to commit, and he wouldn't do it."

"You have a point there," acknowledged Pauline. "He watched what was going on but he didn't lift a finger."

"He was a very passive sort of guy," agreed Marsha.

"He was a bastard," I pronounced vehemently, warming to my point.

"Maybe he just wasn't that interested," noted Herb. "He liked her, only not that much."

"He was interested enough to tell the story," I noted. "He was watching her like a hawk."

"He was curious," said Roger.

"He was a voyeur," said Pauline.

"He was gay," said Philip.

I have to say that Philip's statement seemed a cogent insight, and one that, in the book, as in life, I had missed. Everyone laughed, even Bathsheba and Derek—and Pauline later told me that the gay perspective on the classics had been a great success.

CHAPTER

15

A few weeks after book club, I happened to run into the not-so-wispy Stephen in the mailroom. I'd seen him fleetingly a few times since our encounter at the Doggie Meet and Greet, and he was always in a hurry. Once, I'd seen him leaving the building with an attractive blond, confirming Pauline's suspicion that I had missed my chance. He looked like he was in a hurry today too, and yet he paused long enough to say hello. Now that he appeared to be taken, I could also note that he had a nice smile.

"I'm afraid I've been busy," he said, referring to his absence from book club. This was precisely what I'd said when I believed, fleetingly, that I had found my Prince Charming in the person of Philip. In the lexicon of the New York singles scene, "being busy" obviously means "I've met someone, and going to book club is no longer at the top of my list of things to do." But Stephen, to his credit, did not appear dismissive of me as I had been of him, which says something further for his character and gave me another reason (along with the fact that he had apparently been snapped up by someone else) to think more highly of him than I had before.

"I'm sorry I couldn't make the discussion of *Daisy Miller*," he continued, sounding sincere. "I would have liked to hear what you had to say. I didn't love it, but I read some others in the Henry James collection I have that I liked better. *The Beast in the Jungle*, for example. That really scared me. Have you read it?"

There were a number of things to surprise me in this communication, which happened to be the longest speech I'd heard out of the mouth of the no-longer-wispy-appearing Stephen. First was the fact that he expressed interest in my point of view. No doubt he was just being polite, but since most men couldn't care less about being polite, when you find one who is, you notice. Second was that he'd read beyond the assignment. It brought back the impressive way he had identified a relevant passage in *The Great Gatsby* several months back—clearly, he had a functioning brain, also a novelty. Finally, he was asking about *The Beast in the Jungle*, a story that made a strong impression on me when I read it in college, and which I still think about sometimes when I'm feeling especially bad about my life. (Please note that if you haven't read *The Beast in the Jungle* and think you might ever have the urge to hunker down with a very dense piece of writing that is likely to depress you, you should skip the next paragraph.)

Here's the gist of *The Beast in the Jungle*: There's this guy who thinks he's fated to have something very important happen to him. One day, he meets a woman, and he tells her about this feeling, and she agrees to wait with him to see what it is that will happen. They wait and wait until she finally dies, and when he goes to visit her grave, he suddenly realizes that she was in love with him, and that, if he'd loved her back, *this* could have been the thing he was waiting for. So—his revelation is that he missed his chance, and now what is going to happen to him is a big nothing.

This may sound pretty silly, and a lot of people in my college English class said that it gave them a headache, but it got to me even then, and it's bothered me ever since, making me wonder, for example, if I missed my chance with Bob or Roberto or some other guy I never took seriously. This would include Stephen, who was standing right there in front of me looking much less wispy than I had thought, but whom I hadn't noticed until he was snapped up by someone else—which isn't the same thing as dying, like the woman in the story, but close enough. Any one of these people might have been the love of my life, and, given that, like the guy in the story, I was fated never to realize this until it was too late, I was probably going to have a big nothing happen to me too.

I didn't say this to Stephen, of course, acknowledging only that I knew *The Beast in the Jungle* and yes, I thought it was scary.

"The woman in the story was an idiot," he noted.

Once again, I have to say, I was surprised. It never occurred to me to blame the woman in the story. She always seemed to be the innocent victim of the main character, who couldn't see what was there right in front of his nose. "The woman?" I said now. "Why do you say that?"

"If she loved the guy, she should have told him how she felt and given him a chance to respond."

This was certainly a different angle, and, as I thought about it, there was something to what Stephen said—especially since it had the value of making me feel better. I mean if the woman was to blame for not saying what she felt, then maybe all my disastrous relationships weren't entirely my fault either.

"But maybe I missed the point," Stephen added quickly. "After all, I teach math; literature isn't really my thing."

"Stories like that don't have one point," I noted graciously. This happens to be one of the few practical insights I gained from my overpriced and otherwise useless English degree. "Now that you mention it, the woman was pretty passive."

Stephen seemed pleased that I could see his point, and I think he would have said more, but Pedro told him he had a message and gave him a folded sheet of paper that seemed to distract him—no doubt a note from his new girlfriend, who, given that I was now seeing some value in him, was bound to be there as the inevitable obstacle.

Fortunately, I too was pressed for time. I had to pick up a copy of the *New York Post* for Brodsky (who liked to do close readings of Page 6) and a jar of Sanka for Mrs. Schwartz, who believed that all coffee, with the exception of Sanka (perhaps owing to its unpalatability), was at the center of an insidious capitalistic cartel. I needed to run these errands and get back before the pest control guy was scheduled to arrive. If I missed pest control, I risked a cockroach infestation—precisely the sort of thing that counts as urgent when you live in New York.

CHAPTER

16

Not long after my unfortunate fling with Yves, I called Pauline and mentioned my renewed interest in getting a job in the mayor's office. Yes, it would mean seeing Derek more than I might want, but my desire to get out of the vicinity of air-conditioning engineers, even if it meant replacing them with sanitation workers, had suddenly grown more acute.

Pauline understood immediately, as she always did. She put down the phone and yelled out to Roger, who was apparently in the next room: "You need to get Suzanne an interview for that job we discussed."

"What job?" I heard Roger yell back.

"The one doing negotiation with the sanitation workers," yelled Pauline.

"That wasn't a job," yelled Roger. "I just told you that it was hard to work with the sanitation workers."

"And I told you that you need to hire Suzanne to negotiate with them. She has a real gift. You should have seen how she handled Karen and Iris on the playground."

They were yelling back and forth from different rooms, and I couldn't see why one of them couldn't go to where the other was, especially since I knew that Pauline was on a portable phone, but apparently they liked yelling back and forth. Married people, I'd come to realize, had their own habits, and one shouldn't interfere.

"Listen," Pauline said to me, as there was no response to her last bellow. "I'll have to speak to him about this and get back to you. Don't worry, though; they have plenty of people in that office who do nothing. Derek, for example—I have no idea what he does, and I'm pretty sure it's nothing. Another person isn't going to make a difference. I know it's at the taxpayers' expense, but you can't fix things like this overnight, so you might as well take advantage of them. Besides, you would be a real asset, given your writing and negotiation skills. So let me work on it—he always comes around to my point of view if I nag him enough."

I believed her. Having Pauline work on something was a guarantee that it would get done. She had enormous energy that, no longer focused on a career, spilled over into all walks of life. Rose got the benefit of some of it, but so did the local Reform Synagogue, the ACLU, and her gourmet cooking group—not to mention book club. In the time left over, she managed Roger's career. The mayor himself was known to duck out of the building when he heard she was around, knowing that if she asked him to do something he wouldn't have the nerve to say no.

Unsurprisingly, therefore, I got a call the next day from Roger asking me to drop by the office for an informal interview. "Turns out we do have an opening in the communications area," he said vaguely, "and Pauline thinks you'd be ideal for it."

CHAPTER

17

WHEN I ARRIVED at City Hall I was ushered into an ante-room to wait for someone to meet with me. This someone turned out to be Derek.

"I hope you don't mind if I do the interview," said Derek. "Roger was going to do it, but then I said I really wanted to have a chance to say a few words, given that I'd led you on like I did, and be sure that there were no hard feelings."

I told him there were no hard feelings.

"Bathsheba and I broke up again," said Derek, looking at me plaintively. "You might have noticed that we weren't getting along too well at book club."

I would have had to be catatonic not to have noticed they weren't getting along, but instead I said, "Really? I'm sorry to hear that."

Derek looked at me doubtfully. He clearly did not believe that I was sorry and, rather, was sure I was dying to take him back but didn't want to seem too eager. I felt it best, given that he was interviewing me for a job, not to go out of my way to disabuse him of this notion.

"So . . . the job?" I cued him. "Do you want to hire me? I have excellent communications skills."

"Yes," sighed Derek. "I remember how well you handled the boys."

I was obviously developing something of a reputation in the area of child negotiation, which I assumed translated well into negotiating with recalcitrant labor.

"I'm told there are problems with the sanitation workers," I said, taking the interview into my own hands, since Derek seemed inclined to stall indefinitely on the subject of my handling of his boys. "I happen to have a special expertise in technical communication that might be useful in this area." It had occurred to me that sanitation might come under the rubric of being technical since it was the sort of thing that people didn't want to deal with.

"I see that," said Derek glancing distractedly at my resume. "You look like just the sort of person we could use. I'll talk to Roger, who of course will rubber stamp it, given that it was Pauline's idea to begin with, and then we'll simply have to send it by the assistant deputy mayor, the deputy mayor, and the mayor; then the personnel people, who shouldn't object, especially when they see that this is going to help with the sanitation workers; then, the HR people and the PR people. They have to have a say, given we're talking about something that might make the news— garbage, you know. It's not that they'll have a problem, but they don't like to rush into things. Maybe a month or two, and we should be off and running."

"That long?" I asked surprised.

"Things happen slowly here. It's the public sector. You have to be patient." He gave me the hangdog look that I recalled from our time together. "But it will be great to have you by my side again," he added.

I figured that by the time I was hired Derek might be back with Bathsheba, so I nodded and let him kiss me on the cheek.

"You'll hear from us—eventually," he said.

Pauline called me that night to say that as far as she could see the job was in the bag, but that, as Derek had already explained, the wheels ground exceedingly slow in the public sector. "Chances are that by the time they hire you, the sanitation workers will be on strike, which will be a real challenge, since everyone will really hate each other by then. If I were running the place, it would be different," she noted, perhaps missing the time when she did high-level moving and shaking instead of distributing juice boxes. It occurred to me that one of the benefits for men like Roger and Derek of having women like Pauline consigned to the playground was that the men could now be left alone to do things the way they wanted—which is to say, slowly and not very well.

CHAPTER

18

I WAS NOW in a holding pattern. Before, I'd felt that working for the air-conditioning engineers was my fate. It was not a good job—boring and poorly remunerated—but I had no expectations of anything better. Now, however, my perspective had changed. I sensed that what I had been doing was of the past, while the future would be different, though it had yet to materialize. What was I waiting for? To be honest, I felt like the character in the Henry James story: something large and important seemed to be looming, but a job in the public sector dealing with garbage somehow didn't fit the bill.

I have to say that what *was* waiting in the wings was a real surprise, but not, at least by any obvious measure, a good one. This goes to prove another of Eleanor's dictums: "At our age, there are more bad surprises than good ones. If you want to be surprised, be prepared not to like it." Truer words were never spoken.

My surprise came when I got around to having my yearly gyn appointment with Dr. Laurie McCormack-Stern ("call me Laurie"). Laurie, who looked to be around twenty-two despite her very long name and her degrees from Stanford, the University of Pennsylvania, and Columbia (a pedigree trumpeted by the many framed diplomas on her walls), discovered a lump in my left breast.

I suppose right now you're saying "Whoa—I didn't sign on for this." Well, I'm sorry; I'm not going to leave this out just because it makes you feel bad. How do you think it made me feel? Even Dr. Chitturi couldn't put her usual reverse spin on things, and said only, "Suzanne, this is not good news. But we will deal with it." That was the best she could do, so you can imagine the amount of rummaging I had to do in Eleanor's medicine cabinet to try to calm myself down.

Even after a few Xanaxes and a few drinks, not to mention a half-dozen Reese's Pieces, I was still in a bad state over what the extremely well-trained but disorientingly youthful Laurie had told me: I might have a malignancy (i.e., breast cancer), though then again, I might not. And here I have to tell you something about uncertainty. You haven't experienced the anxiety bred out of uncertainty until you've waited for the results of a biopsy. I thought I had already suffered everything that is possible when it comes to waiting. I had waited for whole weekends at a time, for whole weeks even, for some imagined Mr. Right to call me, only to find out, after I broke down and called him, that he'd gotten back together with his venal ex-girlfriend. I had also had two excruciating weeks when I thought I might be pregnant by Roberto (the then-gig-playing deadbeat, now seven-figure lawyer), imagining a nightmarish scenario in which the baby was raised by my mother and grew up to hate me. But these periods of uncertainty were nothing compared to what I had to face now. I mean, this uncertainty was about whether I was going to die in the near future—and if not in the near future, then in the not-so-near future. If I believed in God—which I don't except when I'm having an anxiety attack and start promising I'll believe in him if he'll just give me a good outcome—I'd say he's one inconsiderate sort of guy, someone who makes those guys who made me wait by the phone while they were getting back together with their venal ex-girlfriends look like paragons of thoughtfulness by comparison.

So let me take you through this as best I can so you get the full flavor of my ordeal. First, Laurie sent me to the surgeon for the biopsy. This surgeon was possibly not entirely human. He had a smooth lusterless complexion that made him seem to be made of wax. He also spoke in a very calm, almost monotone voice, so that you might think you were being dealt with by a well-dressed robot, were it not for his waxy complexion and the fact that his eyes darted around a lot as though he were itching to get his hands on a knife. For the biopsy, however, he had to make due with a very large needle.

"Just a little pinch," he said, injecting said needle into my left breast, "and we'll see what we have going on." He said this as though there might be some sort of wild partying going on in the area of my left breast, and his eyes darted around as though he were looking for a knife that he could grab and put a stop to that festivity then and there.

After the biopsy, I had to wait for the results, which is when I essentially went nuts. I even contemplated calling my mother, but restrained myself, knowing that then it would become not only my hysteria but hers too that we would need to manage. Instead, I went over to Eleanor's and rummaged in her medicine chest while moaning that I was going to die.

Eleanor, fortunately for me, is not the hysterical type. It's probably what drew us together in the fourth grade; we complemented each other. She stayed calm when I went berserk—or, put another way, she made irrational choices sanely, like marrying the sociopathic Ronnie, while I assiduously avoided making choices altogether and then boohooed that my life was going nowhere.

I had stretched out on Eleanor's sofa to sob, while she fed me Cosmopolitans and potato chips with sour cream and onion dip because when you have cancer you don't have to think as much about your weight.

She told me that I would be fine; she knew it; she had an instinct for these things.

A few days later, the biopsy returned to confirm Laurie's suspicion that the lump was malignant.

"You see!" I wailed.

"So you have breast cancer," said Eleanor, recouping. "Everyone gets breast cancer at some point. If you didn't get it now, you'd have to get it later, when you might be doing something really important. This is probably the best time to get it, when you're not involved with anyone and you don't really like your job. You can afford to have it now."

"But if I die, I won't have a chance to meet anyone or get a better job," I whimpered. "Then, it *wouldn't* be a good time."

But Eleanor insisted that my cancer wasn't going to be serious, and even if it was—Eleanor always had a fallback plan—it was going to give me a whole new perspective on things.

"But I don't want a new perspective," I wailed, sprawled on Eleanor's sofa, shoveling the potato chips and sour cream and onion dip into my mouth. "I want to live." I had already begun imagining the slow wasting away—with that window of opportunity when I would be able to wear all those dresses in my closet that pulled around the hips—then the taking to my bed, the parceling out of my few possessions to my few friends, and the final extinction. My only solace was that in the movie, Susan Sarandon managed to look better and better the closer she got to death.

"You can borrow Wordsworth for company," said Eleanor, proving to me that she was indeed a true friend, since as I have already explained, Wordsworth served her as the canine equivalent of Prozac.

I assured her tearfully that borrowing Wordsworth would not be necessary. I would simply visit—as long as I had the strength. Then she would have to come to me, even though my apartment was much smaller.

"Don't be silly," said Eleanor. "You're going to be fine. You'll lose a little weight, meet some cute doctors, get a new lease on life—it's like going to a spa, except with chemo."

I can't say Eleanor sold me on the spa idea, but I did calm down considerably when, after going under the knife of the waxen but wild-eyed surgeon, it was discovered that my cancer was contained to the left breast, that none of the dreaded lymph nodes were involved, and that I was "hormone positive" (hormones being in general a real nuisance, but when it comes to breast cancer, apparently, you want them). In other words, the waxen, wild-eyed surgeon, having gotten the chance to wield his knife, had cut out the cancer, and, as a result, my prognosis was pretty good.

That, at least, was the opinion of the oncologist, Dr. Farber, to whom the surgeon referred me. This individual, occupying the last stop on the cancer train, so to speak, had a thick beard, possibly to make him appear more venerable given his relative youth but which, instead, produced a costumed appearance, as though he had dressed up as a doctor for Halloween and was about to go out trick-or-treating. Dr. Farber discussed my cancer with a jaunty air, which I suppose is understandable, since when you deal with malignant tumors all day long, you are bound to get a little heady when you stumble on a case that isn't a guaranteed death sentence.

"If you're going to have breast cancer, this is the one to have," Dr. Farber announced.

"What does that mean?" I asked suspiciously.

"It means you have a good prognosis."

"And what does that mean?"

"It means that your cancer tends to respond well to treatment."

"And what does that mean?"

"It means there's a good chance of preventing it from coming back."

We went on like this for a while, and when I finally pinned him down, I learned that my particular cancer had about an 80 percent cure rate—in other words, pretty good, which is, when you think about it, the story of my life: blight and misfortune, but of a manageable, relatively harmless sort.

Still, there was an additional issue that had to be addressed with regard to my pretty good cancer before the dancing in the streets could begin.

"There's a test we need to give you if you're an Ashkenazi Jew," Dr. Farber informed me, flipping through my chart. "Are you an Ashkenazi Jew?" He framed this as a question but his tone was more on the order of: "I assume you are an Ashkenazi Jew." He could obviously discern my Semitic lineage, despite the fact that I had far less of the Kaplan nose than the Davis knees—but then, I could discern his through the disguise of his Halloween beard, so we were even. When I acknowledged that I was an Ashkenazi Jew, he told me I would be obliged to take a "Barack test"—at least, that's what it sounded like, and for a moment I thought he was telling me that he only treated Jews who supported Obamacare (which might seem bizarre, but in New York you couldn't rule such things out).

As it happened, however, he'd said "Braca," not "Barack," which is how you pronounce the BRCA test used to ascertain whether you have a certain gene, common in Eastern European Jews, that lets you know if you are likely to get more of whatever cancer it is you have (and let's face it, cancer, even if it's pretty good cancer, isn't something you want to have more of). I spent two weeks popping Xanax (I now had my own stash) before I learned that I did not have said deadly gene, which meant, in a nutshell, that my pretty good cancer was going to stay that way (though of course, as Dr. Farber made sure to tell me, to protect himself from liability, there were no guarantees).

With my BRCA test out of the way, Dr. Farber and I met again to address my treatment regimen. He explained that I would be given twenty weeks of chemotherapy, followed by five weeks of radiation, and, to top things off, five years on the oral medication tamoxifen to prevent recurrence. Wonderful stuff, tamoxifen, with the one drawback that, while taking it, one could not, under any circumstances, get pregnant. Dr. Farber explained this precisely and relentlessly: "There are less good cancers that don't respond to tamoxifen, which means that some women may have a poorer general prognosis but a better chance to procreate. You have a better general prognosis and a poorer chance to procreate." In short, even my pretty good cancer wasn't going to cut me any slack.

CHAPTER

19

You're probably asking yourself where my mother was in all this—a good question, and one that was on my mind. Part of me had wanted to pick up the phone and wail to her as soon as my gyn had found the lump; but another part of me, the rational part, knew this wasn't a good idea. To get my mother involved would be to add a whole new layer of drama to my ordeal. She would have promptly usurped my breast cancer and made it *our* breast cancer, which meant that she would have hauled me to every cancer mecca in the country, consulted every specialist that her friend's son, some big-cheese urologist, recommended, and looked into every hare-brained protocol that she had read about in those health-food magazines. The very thought of her co-opting my breast cancer and all the exertion that would ensue made me want to take to my bed right then and there.

Fortunately, I was not able to succumb to contacting my mother since she was off on a cruise. It so happens that the over-fifty-five community where my mother lives in Santa Fe, New Mexico, goes in for strenuous activities that remind me of an Outward Bound program, and their latest excursion was a month-long jaunt to Athens, Istanbul, and the Greek Islands. However at odds the Greeks and Turks have historically been, I could at least thank them for, together, diverting my mother from meddling with me. Eventually, I knew, she would return, and I would have to tell her, which would result in tempestuous scenes in which she would berate me for the months in which she could have been worrying about me but wasn't. But that was in the future. For now, I could concentrate on my pretty good cancer without having to contend with her concentrating on it too.

You'd think that my condition would have made me sink into total despondency. Truth be told, it did not. I wept and wailed, don't get me wrong, but when I was done, I was OK, a fact that I put down at first to finally having something concrete to complain about. I mean when you've been complaining that your life sucks every day of the year but can't put your finger on exactly what it is that bums you out, it helps that now, when someone asks, "How ya doing?" you can say, "Not too good. I have cancer." No one is going to begrudge you a little complaining about that.

But I also realized that it wasn't only that I finally had something substantial to complain about; it was that I could see, for the first time, how much I *didn't* have to complain about. Sappy as it sounds, it was the perspective thing that Eleanor had predicted; it was kicking in. Confronted with my mortality, all those routine, everyday activities that had weighed on me took on a certain lightness, even piquancy. This is my life, I told myself. It's not exactly what I had in mind, granted, but it has its points. I can feel the wind on my face as I walk down Broadway, eat a bowl of buttered popcorn while watching *CSI* (to which, thanks to the recommendation of the Rosenbaums, I had become addicted), stretch out on Eleanor's couch and listen to her berate the sociopathic Ronnie, and regale the boys at I-ACE with the stories of my life, which now included some colorful ones about the ins and outs of cancer treatment. It was amazing how a suspended death sentence can bathe one's world in a softer glow. I even started thinking that, cancer or no cancer, we all have to die eventually and should therefore relish being alive for the short time we are allotted. If, prior to my diagnosis, someone had voiced this idea in my presence, I would have judged said person to be an annoying goody-goody, but since the idea was now mine, I found it profound. There's a lesson in that.

Along with the philosophical stuff that I'd started thinking about, I'd also gotten into the habit of enumerating more specific things for which I was thankful: 1) that I had health insurance; 2) that I had a friend who was supportive without being lachrymose; 3) that my prognosis was pretty good.

On the down side, of course, there were a couple of issues that I felt obliged to face, first and foremost the cancer itself. I mean, you can't entirely sugarcoat that. From this fact, a number of unfortunate corollaries followed: 1) that I would now have to spend lots of time getting treatment (which, along with possible pain and discomfort, would mean sitting in waiting rooms watching the television positioned on some unreachable perch and perennially tuned to *The View*); 2) that my hair would fall out; and 3) that the treatment might impede my ability to procreate.

But even these negatives had a silver lining, as it turned out. Going for treatment, for example, didn't really bother me. What else had I got to do anyway? I also happened to like *The View*, and where, in the past, I felt guilty watching it, I now had no choice—everyone getting chemo had to watch it, almost as though it were part of the treatment.

As for my hair falling out, I decided to see this as a cosmetic opportunity. I had never liked my hair. It was bushy and unmanageable, and I had often envied Orthodox Jewish women who struck me as having their looks improved by glossy, good-quality wigs. I looked forward to going with Eleanor to a wig store she knew in the West Village where she was prepared to buy me an early birthday present. There was also the promise that, if everything went according to plan and my pretty good cancer didn't turn out to be less good than was thought, my hair would grow back and, according to the oncologist, be softer and more manageable than it was now. In other words, one of the perks of having cancer was that you could end up with better hair.

Admittedly, Number 3 on my negatives list, the fertility thing, struck me at first as a real bummer. How had I managed to contract my pretty good cancer at the worst possible age? By the time I finished taking the tamoxifen, I would be forty years old, the end of my childbearing years. "It is a case of unfortunate timing," as the hirsute oncologist put it, which seemed to imply that there were people who managed to time their cancer well. Yet the fact is, I didn't feel as bad about my timing as I would have expected. It had the value of taking the responsibility for my biological clock out of my hands. That clock had, for the past few years, been ticking very loudly—so loudly, in fact, that it had given me a splitting headache. To have the ticking stop was something of a relief. I could hear again: the cars honking in the stalled traffic, the garbage men throwing the cans around outside my window, the deafening clatter of the subway pulling into my station—all that cacophony of life that had been drowned out by my infernal biological ticktock. It was such a pleasure to hear the world again, and my sense of relief was so great, that I even bypassed the chance to freeze my eggs. If having a child of my own was not meant to be, then it was not meant to be. There were all those starving children in Africa, not to mention all those potential genius children in China who, once I had kicked my pretty good cancer, I could adopt.

I had decided not to keep my cancer a secret, given that I have a hard time keeping secrets, and anyway I figured I might as well reap the benefits of my condition. There are very few instances in life when you get a free pass, and having cancer is one of them. I mean if I'd won a Pulitzer Prize, been elected to a high office, or finished a stint in the Peace Corps, I imagine that people would treat me well—but such things require a good deal of effort. Here, with no exertion whatsoever, I found myself in an elevated position that garnered me a tremendous amount of goodwill. Friends suddenly seemed inclined to pick up the check (this struck me as mildly illogical, since if I am going to die soon, I am the one with the greater disposable income).

When I announced my condition during one of my irregular visits to I-ACE headquarters, the response was beyond my expectations. Walt took out his dirty handkerchief and began furiously wiping his eyes. "This is too much," he muttered. "You are the light of my life, Suzanne."

The idea that I was the light of Walt's life gave me pause. First of all, I come in on a very irregular basis, which means that Walt must spend most of his time in the dark, and second, when I do come in, I rarely say more than two words to Walt. Yet those two words, uttered very sporadically, obviously meant a lot to him. This was flattering, and buoyed my spirits for the rest of the day.

Dave, too, looked shaken. He told me that his sister had succumbed to breast cancer, and for me to have it too was hard for him to bear. He looked at me as though I were already dead, but with so much compassion that I felt that it was he not me who ought to be consoled.

Even Roy seemed disturbed by my news, and Roy is an absolutely even-keeled person who, you have to assume, is at least borderline autistic. He said that he would have his mother cook me some of her strudel—for Roy, strudel was the height of sensual pleasure, given that all other sources of pleasure were entirely forbidden in the maternal home.

I had to assure the guys that my prognosis was pretty good but that if my work was a bit more erratic than usual, it was only because the regimen of treatment was taking its toll. I-ACE work was not, as you may already have gleaned, particularly taxing, but the national convention to be held in Parsippany was approaching, and I had a sheaf of technical papers on my desk at home that were waiting to be translated into press releases to be ignored by the media. I figured I might as well take advantage of my diagnosis and ease whatever strain this task might place on me.

The guys were extremely supportive. I was told that I shouldn't think twice about work. "It's only air conditioning," said Walt in a philosophical aside.

"Concentrate on getting well," said Dave. "That's your job now. We can handle the indoor-air-quality press releases, if necessary."

"I'll have the strudel for you next week," said Roy, as though this, more than chemo or any expert medical care, was sure to cure me.

CHAPTER

20

A SUBSTANTIAL OUTPOURING of sympathy also came from the playground mothers, several of whom had had relatives with breast cancer, not to mention run-ins of their own with the disease, and were therefore full of advice. Everyone seemed genuinely concerned, since no taint of competition regarding children, income, or work versus home was present in my situation to muddy the waters. Indeed, one saw the best in these women as they rallied to my side. Suddenly I felt that they were all my new best friends.

In no time, an entire assembly line of meals had been organized by Pauline to be delivered to me every night for an indeterminate period. I told them not to bother—that I didn't usually eat dinner in any formal sense and lived primarily on salad, leftover Chinese food from dinners out, and Lean Cuisines. This, however, only intensified the sense among the mothers that I needed to be taken on as their overgrown new child. It was everyone's conviction that a three-course cooked dinner was absolutely necessary to help me beat my pretty good cancer.

I also got a call from my friends NateandClara—I think of them this way because they met during their freshman year in college and sort of became one person. NateandClara had moved to Edison, New Jersey, about a year ago so they could live in something bigger than a shoebox and maybe start a family. They liked to call me from time to time to discuss how much they missed New York and whether they should finish their basement. Possibly in order to avoid the latter topic, I told them about my pretty good cancer, which meant that they immediately informed my friends Miriam and Carlos in Westchester (who, since he was in hedge funds and she was in arbitrage, had already finished their basement and even had a few kids rattling around in it). Miriam told Meredith in Hoboken, so that somehow Yuri and Dustin, who live in not-very-nice parts of Brooklyn, not to mention a few other people who live in relative squalor on the Lower East Side, got wind of it, with the result that one day all of the above showed up at my apartment with a jar of jelly beans, a large moose-like stuffed animal, and a Kindle loaded with what NateandClara informed me were my favorite books. How could I not be touched? I had no idea these people liked me enough to come up with such an exceptional triumvirate of gifts. I mean the jar of jelly beans even had the black licorice ones in there, which you don't see much of nowadays and which I happen to be partial to, and the moose was really cute (you may be surprised that I like stuffed animals, but I happen to keep a bunch of them under my bed, a fact that I thought only Eleanor knew). As for the Kindle, although I had just bad-mouthed this device to the playground mothers as the death of civilization, I secretly wanted one, and was impressed to see that NateandClara actually knew some of my favorite books, though they were dead wrong on others, excuse the pun. (I am not, I repeat *not*, a David Foster Wallace fan.)

Faced with these people at my door, I had to hold back tears and assure everyone that their gifts were unwarranted, especially since I was going to have to disappoint them and not die—a statement that got even more of a laugh than it deserved.

Pedro, who learned about my illness via Pauline, also informed the old Jews. I was still making my rounds with these individuals, even though, technically speaking, I was no longer needed; the urinating dog having been identified, Pedro had resumed his former schedule. Still, I decided to keep up my own visits, since everyone knows that the elderly need continuity, and I didn't want to be responsible for having them go into a tailspin of depression or disorientation if I suddenly stopped appearing in their lives. I had also become mildly curious about the next outlandish thing that would come out of their mouths.

Anyway, when the old Jews learned about my plight, I received their version of sympathy. The Rosenbaums lent me the first season of *The Wire*, which, they said, with all its shooting and drug dealing, would help take my mind off my own death—it had worked for them. Only I should be sure to return it.

When I visited Brodsky, he responded in character.

"What's this about your having cancer?" he asked. "I'm the one who's supposed to have cancer."

"Excuse me for dying," I said.

This caused Brodsky to say nothing, a behavior so unusual that I felt constrained to add, "Actually, I'm not dying. My cancer happens to be curable. I'll be fine."

"Glad to hear it," said Brodsky huskily. Then, rallying, "I hope they don't have to cut off your boobs."

"Unlikely," I said, "but you don't like them much anyway."

"You're putting words in my mouth. I only said they were OK, not great. Of course, if they cut them off, you could get better ones."

"That's true," I admitted.

"Not that the ones you have are bad."

"So you've explained."

"But there's always better. You could get a size or two bigger. Bigger is always better."

"I'll keep that in mind. Though I don't think it's going to be necessary."

"Good." This, to my mind, was both a huge compliment and an outpouring of sentiment where Brodsky was concerned.

As for Mrs. Schwartz, she told me that she'd had the Big C fifty years ago. "Lopped off both of them," she said pointing to her chest area, which was swaddled in a house dress and a cardigan—maybe two cardigans, it was hard to say; the effect was very layered. "In those days, they didn't think twice about it. Just cut you up. Typical capitalist brutality. Especially when it came to women. We were a dime a dozen. Mort, God bless him, said I was woman enough, even without them." She peered at me a moment in what I construed as some semblance of sympathy. "But you're not married yet, are you?" she asked. "Not all men are like Mort."

I told her that that was true but that the point was not really relevant since I didn't need a mastectomy.

"The men these days may be better," said Mrs. Schwartz, ignoring what I'd said. "Though I doubt it. Men like Mort don't come around very often." She again looked at me thoughtfully. "You're better off without a man, especially if they cut them off."

I repeated that I doubted this would be necessary, the cutting that is, but that I'd take her view of men under advisement.

"There's a talk on Emma Goldman at the 92nd Street Y next week," she noted in an abrupt transition. "I thought we could go together."

Mrs. Schwartz almost never went out, and that she would propose such a thing meant that she either was very interested in the topic or very sorry for me.

"It's impressive that she wants to go with you," Pedro said when I told him. "But you might want to take a rain check, given your cancer and all. Mrs. Schwartz is kind of hard to maneuver." Frankly, I think he was jealous. He was her boychik.

"Of course, I'll go," I said regally. "I'm not incapacitated, you know. And besides, I'm very interested in Emma Goldman"—though actually, I had no idea who she was until I looked her up on Wikipedia.

A WEEK OR SO after the diagnosis, I also got a call from Derek.

"I heard about your breast cancer," he said. "I thought maybe I could do something."

I wondered what it could be he thought he could do, given that he was neither a doctor nor a social worker. Having shown himself to be strikingly inept in dealing with his children, it seemed unlikely that he could deal with me should I find myself in extremis—but I let it pass. I assured him that I had a pretty good support system and a pretty good cancer.

"I'm glad to hear that," he said wistfully. "Bathsheba had a scare a few years ago, so I've been through it, at least hypothetically. As you know, she and I are no longer together, so I'd have time to help you out if you need it."

I assured him that I didn't.

"I know I treated you badly," said Derek, "and that it hurt you a lot, but I'm ready to make it up now."

I assured him that there was nothing to make up. I harbored no ill feelings. I was, however, busy right now, with the chemo and the upcoming air-conditioning-engineers convention.

"Maybe in a while, when you're feeling better," he said. "We're hoping that your job will be approved soon. There's a delay, you know, because of the budget shortfall, but in a few months, things should be on track again."

I said that sounded good. By then, my cancer treatment would be near completion and I'd be able to devote myself to ending the sanitation strike that would undoubtedly be in full swing.

"It's OK if you need time off for your treatment," Derek assured me. "We have a very good disability plan." Apparently, I could take off even before I had been hired. "I should tell you," added Derek hesitatingly. He now seemed intent on broaching a delicate subject: "Breasts aren't that important to me."

I told him I was pleased to hear it—obviously, Mrs. Schwartz was being proved wrong—but that this was not an issue for me since a mastectomy would not be necessary. If things changed—with my breasts or anything else—I would keep him in mind.

CHAPTER

21

Now that I had gone under the knife, it was time to move on to the next phase of treatment, which was the chemo. Frankly, I would have liked to skip this phase. Didn't I have a good-sized dent in my left breast to prove that the cancer had been cut out, and hadn't the wild-eyed surgeon, who was nothing if not thorough, promised me that he had gotten it all? But when I asked Dr. Farber if maybe I could bypass the chemo, he said no, absolutely not; the chemo was non-negotiable. You had to have it because you couldn't trust the cancer to accept that it was out of the picture just because someone had gone after it with a knife. No. The cancer was stubborn and sly. You had to zap it with toxic chemicals and deadly radiation, and even then you couldn't be sure it got the message and wouldn't wheedle its way back—sort of like those guys who break up with you but then end up calling you in the middle of the night a year later. You think that maybe they've realized that you are the love of their life and that they can't live without you, but really they're just bored and enjoy knowing that they still can make you miserable.

Not an exact analogy to cancer, I grant you, but not altogether off the mark either.

To prepare for the chemo, Dr. Farber scheduled me for an information session where I would learn all the ins and outs associated with kicking the crap out of my cancer. He recommended that I have someone accompany me to this session because, as he put it, "it's good to have a second pair of ears." It was hard for me to tell with Dr. Farber, given that his beard covered most of his face, whether this was standard procedure and all his patients were poor listeners or whether he had doubts about me in particular. If the latter, he would not have been wrong. Despite my job as a technical writer (which is a misnomer anyway), I am not good with facts. One of the reasons I majored in English was because there wasn't very much in the way of concrete information that I had to learn; I could say anything and it wouldn't be wrong. But start loading me down with lots of facts in a very short time and my mind is going to wander—and that's without cancer. With it, there's no telling how flaky I would become.

Fortunately, Eleanor agreed to accompany me to the information session. Eleanor happens to be good with facts, which is one of the reasons why we found each other in the fourth grade: she did the research for the report on the Westward Movement, and I wrote all the flowery stuff about the hardships of the pioneer women and drew the picture of the wagon train for the cover.

So Eleanor and I went to Dr. Farber's office, where he introduced us to his nurse practitioner, Abigail Wu, whose job, he said, was to do the explaining. A nurse practitioner, from what I can make out, is someone who knows more or less the same stuff as the doctor but has more patience for explaining it. It was clear at once that Abigail Wu, a small woman in an Eileen Fisher shift dress, was perfect for this job. She was one of those unflappable, quietly rational people to whom you might not pay much attention under ordinary circumstances but who really comes in handy when you have cancer. Had I, for example, suddenly decided to strip off my clothes and run around the room screaming hysterically "Why me? Why me?" Abigail Wu would have waited for me to calm down and continued where she left off.

Abigail Wu led us to a special room that had been fitted out with pictures of sandy beaches and botanical prints. Everyone knows that sandy beaches and botanical prints are supposed to be calming, which, if you're embarking on chemotherapy, can have the opposite effect by making you aware that someone wants you to be calm. A more subtle oncologist might have had pictures of insects and clowns to give the impression that there was nothing to worry about. But you can't expect someone who's spent half his life studying things like the lymphatic system or the growth of solid tumors to understand the subtleties of reverse psychology.

After we had settled into the cluster of cushy chairs that had been arranged in feng shui fashion in the corner and Abigail had served us the prerequisite herbal tea, she handed me a "welcome packet" containing "information about my breast cancer and the many products and services associated with it." I can't say I was thrilled to get the welcome packet. I know firsthand through my work at I-ACE that welcome packets are usually a waste of everyone's time. They tend to contain lots of brochures and fact sheets on overpriced paper that eventually just clutter up your apartment. There's usually one telephone number in some remote corner of one of the brochures that is actually useful but that you can't find when you need it anyway. Eleanor must have known that I was thinking negatively about the welcome packet, because she took it from me and put it into her Kate Spade handbag (purchased, if I may digress for a moment, as a consolation gift for herself soon after she learned of the unseemly goings on of the sociopathic Ronnie). I have to say that the placement of the welcome packet in the Kate Spade handbag had a soothing effect on me—don't ask me why.

Abigail went on to explain the fine points of my regimen, which would consist of four treatments of two toxic chemicals every two weeks, followed by twelve treatments of another toxic chemical once a week, followed by six weeks of toxic radiation on a daily basis. Toxicity here, it goes without saying, was to be directed at the cancer and not at me, though obviously some spillover was to be expected, which was why I would also start on a half dozen other drugs intended to combat the toxicity of said spillover. The names of these other drugs were batted around, but I couldn't tell you what they were because I'd stopped paying attention. Eleanor was furiously jotting everything into her Kate Spade personal planner bought, along with her Kate Spade wallet, Kate Spade change purse, and Kate Spade key chain, at the same time that she laid out 2 G's for the Kate Spade handbag. The thought of all that Kate Spade got me daydreaming about the Prada knock-off that I should have bought before the vendor, who used to elude the police in the East 50s, finally got snagged and deported back to Nigeria. I was regretting the loss of that bag in particular and the crackdown on knock-off vendors in general while Abigail Wu moved on to a discussion of the side effects of the drugs to prevent side effects, and what drugs I could take to prevent those side effects. Chemo drugs and designer names were getting pretty mixed up in my head at this point, but from the little I could make out, the information session boiled down to a very long list of unpleasant things that could happen, though hopefully wouldn't, but which, after all, make sense to think about when a truckload of chemicals are being pumped into your system in order to kill something that's out to kill you.

I was trying to remember the hardware on the knock-off Prada that had slipped through my fingers while Abigail covered such unlikely eventualities as bladder bleeding, mouth sores, acne, and diarrhea, and I had just imagined myself jetting off to Nigeria to peruse the stash of knock-offs that the deported vendor was no doubt keeping in storage in his native village, when we arrived at the concluding topic of the information session: wigs. Wigs were the mecca to which the information session had been wending its way. Wigs were something a cancer patient could look forward to. Sure, to get there you had to lose your hair ("in clumps," as Abigail pointed out, "which can be disturbing"), but wigs were the silver lining. They inserted a little liveliness into these otherwise macabre proceedings. Eleanor and Abigail now discussed the subject with relieved animation, segueing into issues like human hair versus synthetic, and whether short or long would frame my face better. There was also much give-and-take on the merits of Wig-a-Little in the Village, which would accept the discount coupon in my welcome packet, and the more upscale Henri Pierre Human Hair Boutique on the Upper East Side, which wouldn't. I, however, was not involved in this discussion. I had forgotten all about the Prada knock-off and the Nigerian vendor, and was staring at the woman in a head scarf smiling out at me from the welcome packet sticking out of Eleanor's Kate Spade bag.

The next day, I revisited the wild-eyed surgeon for the insertion of the Infuse-a-Port, a plastic doodad placed under the skin near my right clavicle into which the chemo would be pumped. The Infuse-a-Port gave me a cyborgian look in my tighter sweaters and balanced the dent on my left side where the wild-eyed surgeon had perhaps gotten a little carried away with the lumpectomy. Any aspirations I may have harbored to become Playmate of the Month were out the window, but Eleanor, who can always find a bright side, noted that guys like gadgets, and the Infuse-a-Port would make a good conversation piece.

CHAPTER

22

Wʜᴇɴ ʏᴏᴜ ɢᴏ for chemo, you get to take comparative thinking to a new level. I mean here I was with my pretty good cancer thrown in with people whose cancer wasn't so good and some whose cancer wasn't good at all. We all sat there in the chemo chairs and chatted about this and that—sometimes our cancers and sometimes things like problems with our health insurance, the pros and cons of different anti-nausea medicines, and what had really killed Michael Jackson.

I got to know these people fairly well even though under normal circumstances I wouldn't have said two words to them, which opens the world up a bit, as you can imagine. I had already had a taste of this sort of thing with my "giving back" to the old Jews, but this was a whole new level of expanding my horizons. The old Jews were in their way familiar—they were sort of like people in my family, especially the Kaplan side, where there are some real doozies, as my mother likes to say. The people here, however, weren't like anyone in my family. One of the regulars, for example, was a Viet Nam vet named Flanagan with lung cancer, whose principal complaint was that he couldn't smoke. He voiced this complaint continuously and with good humor, although he had only half a voice box with which to do so. We even got into the habit of asking him, "Flanagan, do you want a cigarette?" to which his scripted response was, "I'm dying for one"—which made us all practically roll on the floor with laughter. Really, you had to be there.

Another regular on my schedule was Mrs. Dryer, an elderly African-American woman with ovarian cancer whose husband, until the onset of his wife's illness, didn't know how to turn on the oven but had since become a domestic paragon, cooking meals from scratch and hovering over his wife with cups of tea and snacks. It was such a case of devotion that we all watched with awe—no one had ever seen a man like that; he even sat patiently beside her as she watched her favorite soap opera. Eleanor, who accompanied me to some of my treatments, said that Mr. Dryer had renewed her faith in men, though she suspected that he was a one of a kind model or, given his advanced age, a model that had been retired years ago.

And then there was Ellen Pontillo. You would have had to have a heart of stone not to be wrung out by this forty-six-year-old mother of three, with a third recurrence of breast cancer that had metastasized to her liver—which was as good as saying that she'd be dead in four months, or so I gleaned in an Internet search that I trust Ellen Pontillo had not done. Still, she knew what the score was. You could tell by the way she looked at her kids. This wasn't just looking at them—which, believe me, I've seen Pauline and Karen and Iris do practically all the time this was looking at them because you don't know how much longer you're going to be able to see them. She also cried softly on occasion, and her husband, a big burly guy who was a fireman or possibly a plumber, patted her hand. Still, overall, she was cheerful and, with Mrs. Dryer, was a big fan of *Days of Our Lives*, which the two of them could talk about earnestly for hours. It was a wonder that someone whose life was a soap opera could get so engrossed in a soap opera, but there you are.

It's hard to explain how, with all this death and dying, the atmosphere in Dr. Farber's chemo room wasn't depressing, but I have to say that it wasn't. It helped that Mary Lou and Aidah, Dr. Farber's oncology nurses, were so upbeat, not only in the face of their patients' condition but in the face of their own lives, which I became pretty well versed in and which weren't exactly a bed of roses. Mary Lou was a chunky blond from Mississippi, and Aidah a small, wiry black woman from the West Indies. Both had abysmal love lives, which they recounted to us in an admirably coordinated fashion. One would be accessing the Infuse-a-Port and starting the chemo, while the other would be deep into the latest saga of egregious wrongdoing on the part of some ne'er-do-well man who had attached himself unaccountably to her. Mary Lou had been in a series of bad relationships that dated from childhood. Her father was an alcoholic with a vicious temper from whom she had run away with a local boy who turned out to be an alcoholic with a vicious temper. She had left him for a dentist from New Jersey who, after a year, had shown himself, too, to be an alcoholic with a vicious temper. She was now living with a man in Brooklyn who managed to have a vicious temper without the assistance of alcohol.

As for Aidah, her difficulty involved getting the men who fastened onto her to get off her couch. "I don't know what it is about me," she said, "but these men, they sleep a lot." Initially, she explained, they at least gave her a good time in bed, but soon they didn't even do that, complaining that they were too tired.

"Why he so tired?" Aidah asked in her Jamaican lilt, with regard to her latest ne'er-do-well boyfriend, looking around at us, attached to our IVs, as though we might supply her with the answer. "You people, you got cancer; you not so tired. What he do to be so tired? And why my couch he have to be so tired on?"

These were rhetorical questions, but ones we were none-theless pleased to contemplate. It was a mystery why Mary Lou and Aidah could not, as they put it, find themselves a good man.

"I'm not looking for a Mr. Dryer," Mary Lou explained, motioning to this saintly creature stationed next to his wife, holding her pocketbook. "I'm realistic. I just want someone who won't give me a black eye."

Aidah and Mary Lou were, as they themselves would admit, conditioned into taking care of abusive and deadbeat men, so that coming to work, where they took care of genu-inely sick people, was a liberating and invigorating activity. This gave them a pleasant, upbeat demeanor. And since there was always a new episode in their sagas, there was always something to look forward to when I went for chemo. For the last two sessions, for example, Mary Lou had been dis-cussing the male nurse she had met a few weeks ago, with whom she had felt some definite chemistry.

"A male nurse! They the only good men out there," ex-claimed Aidah when this subject was raised. "Except Mr. Dryer," she qualified, nodding to this individual, who was unwrapping the tinfoil from his wife's vanilla wafers. "You got to be kind and caring to be a nurse. Mary Lou and me, we kind and caring—but with low self-esteem. But a male nurse, he got to have high self-esteem, what with the broth-ers all on him about it. I say you get yourself one of those, you set for life."

I heard a lot about Mary Lou's male nurse because I spent a lot of time in Dr. Farber's office, even between chemo treatments. For example, there were the times I would get queasy and stop eating (which normally I would have embraced as a good thing, but when you have cancer, you want to eat) and had to go in for an extra infusion of anti-nausea meds and some cans of those power drinks to beef me up. Or I'd need some expert advice on constipation and have to consult Aidah and Mary Lou about stool softeners (the old Jews were also helpful on this topic and had strong opinions on the flavors of Metamucil). Or I'd fall behind with the gallons of Gatorade I was supposed to drink and have to come in for IV fluids. In short, the meds to prevent side effects were not altogether effective, side effects managing to creep in anyway, and Dr. Farber's office became like the local Starbucks, where you drop in for a cappuccino (or in this case, an IV infusion) and hang out for a while with the locals.

Most of my time, however, was spent in my apartment, sleeping. I mean I'd sleep for twelve hours and then wake up and need a nap. Eleanor said that I was making up for all the years I'd been a chronic insomniac, and, given that I'd probably be a chronic insomniac again, this was money in the bank. I have to say that it struck me as paradoxical that just when I'd started to get out of my pajamas and get a life, I was now being roped back into staying in my pajamas and sleeping most of the day. Still, I knew there was a difference between this sort of sleep, the product of toxic chemicals meant to discourage my cancer and hence save my life, and the other sort of sleep that I used to do, which was the product of depression and inertia. Yes, I was tired, but oddly, I wasn't depressed or inert. I knew that life was out there waiting for me and that I needed to get well so I could live it.

CHAPTER

23

Eventually, of course, the inevitable happened: my mother returned from her cruise through the Greek Isles and called. Along with telling me about the beauties of ancient Greek culture and how much it had inspired her, she also asked me how I was.

This in itself was not unusual. My mother calls and asks me how I am practically all the time. If the phone rings at 6:30 in the morning when I have finally fallen asleep after spending half the night watching infomercials, it's my mother asking how I am. And if the phone rings at 11:30 at night when I happen to collapse into a few hours of fitful slumber before waking up at 2 A.M. to finish the Häagen Dazs and Google people I didn't like in junior high school, it is my mother asking how I am. She calls at these sorts of hours in order to be sure to get me, since if she does not get me, this puts her "into a state"—i.e., a state of hysteria wondering what I'm doing that could possibly prevent me from answering the phone. This is rather odd, since the reason she usually calls is to find out if I've gotten my life started—which should mean doing something of which answering her phone calls would get in the way. I've tried to explain that she can call my cell phone, but she refuses to do this because 1) she doesn't believe that cell phones are real phones; and 2) she doesn't want to interrupt me if I happen to be chatting up the pharmacist in the Duane Reade or making eyes at the Orthodox Jew in the electronics store—these being the sorts of things I imagine she thinks I should be doing.

But I have not been telling you about my mother's calls for the reason that, though they are frequent, they don't last very long, with my end usually going something like this:

"Yes, Mom, I'm fine. Yes, work is going well. Yes, I'm dating. No, no one in particular. Yes, I'll keep you posted. Yes, I'd be glad to have Sylvia's son's nephew's friend call if he's in town."

I try to keep my responses short and positive because if I don't, my mother will be incited to get involved and, in the process, drive me crazy. I know this, having seen what she did to my father, who though patient up to a point, could only take so much and would end up screaming at the top of his lungs. This made for an extremely fraught environment in which to grow up, as Dr. Chitturi has pointed out on numerous occasions. "You grew up in a war zone, Suzanne," she tells me, "which was very hard for someone with your sensitive nature. But it has given you excellent survival skills that will serve you well once we get the post-traumatic stress out of the way." As you see, Dr. Chitturi manages to acknowledge what I went through while deriving something positive from it—which is why I go to her even though my insurance only pays 20 percent of her fee.

So, as I said, when my mother calls we go through the standard litany of my being fine, etc., etc. I was able to keep this patter up through my second chemo session and might have gotten through the whole regimen without her suspecting anything if it hadn't been my bad luck to have her call when I had just come out of the shower and a whole clump of my hair had fallen out of my head. It's one thing not to like your hair, another to see it disappear in a swirl down the drain and realize that it won't be around much longer for you to complain about. In short, my mother had gotten me at a bad moment.

"What's wrong?" she said. My mother is not a sensitive person, but she is, after all, a mother and has that hawkish maternal ability to discern that you're on the verge of hysteria even when you're trying your best to hide it.

"Nothing," I said. "I'm fine."

"Something's wrong. I can hear it in your voice."

I have always been a terrible liar, which is probably why I have had such limited success with men. Lying is, as far as I can see, one of the primary requisites to being attractive to men: you have to appear cheerful, interested, and full of zest for life—only when the ring is on your finger can you let down your guard and reveal that you are, in actuality, depressed, easily bored, and inclined to sleep until noon.

"I'm fine, really," I said weakly.

"What's wrong?"

"Nothing."

"What's wrong?"

"Mom!"

"Tell me."

"My hair is falling out."

"Get a good conditioner. It will give you more body."

"No, Mom. I mean it. My hair is falling out . . . from chemotherapy. I have breast cancer."

There was silence. It wasn't exactly what she'd been expecting, but to her credit, she did recover quickly and set things in motion. She didn't even stop to castigate me for not having told her earlier.

"I'm packing my bags right now," she announced.

"No, Mom," I said. "Please don't come. It's not a bad cancer. In fact, it's a pretty good cancer: no nodes involved, hormone positive. No reason to be alarmed."

"My daughter has cancer and you say there's no reason to be alarmed!" She said this as though I were a third party who was minimizing access to her daughter with cancer.

"Mother," I said, "I don't want you to come."

"I don't care what you want. I'm coming."

And there you have it: our relationship in a nutshell. Even though I was the one with cancer and I didn't want her to come, she was, nonetheless, coming, because—that's what *she* wanted. The whole situation struck me as a variation on one of those MasterCard commercials: *dead-end job—bad; nonexistent romantic life—worse; cancer—worst; mother coming to take care of you—unmitigated disaster.*

As I've tried to explain, I don't think my mother actually means to do harm. She just has no sense at all that another person with an independent will exists on the other end of her ministrations. It has occurred to me that this might be an undescribed strain of autism. Autistic people have no sense of an emotional life either in themselves or others. People like my mother have no sense that anyone *but* themselves has an emotional life. Dr. Chitturi has pointed out that this is also the definition of narcissism, so maybe autism is narcissism with only one side activated. I've told Dr. Chitturi that she can have this observation if she wants it, maybe to write up for the American Psychological Association or something.

AFTER MY MOTHER announced she was packing her bags and flying out immediately, I barely had a chance to run over to the East Side for a pep talk from Eleanor before she arrived. My mother is that fast. One minute, Eleanor and I are walking Wordsworth in Central Park, where he is growling at the other wheaten terriers and halfheartedly chasing squirrels, and the next minute, my mother is calling up over my intercom, "Yoo-hoo! I'm here!"

She arrived with a suitcase full of the sorts of things she always brings, things that seem expressly designed to irritate me. One of these is a Cuisinart to make me healthy fruit drinks. I hate healthy fruit drinks and have told her so a thousand times. Yet she persists in ignoring my having said this and pushes the stuff on me as though we had never discussed it before. Our conversation invariably goes like this:

"Look what I made you: a nice banana, orange, and strawberry smoothie. It's very refreshing. You'll love it."

"Mom, I don't like fruit smoothies."

"You don't?"

"Mom, you've known me for thirty-four years. Don't you know that by now?"

"Give it a try. It's healthy and delicious."

"Mom, I've tried it. I don't like it."

"Just a little taste."

"No, I won't like it."

"You'd be surprised."

"I said no!"

"Well, you don't have to raise your voice!"

We've had this conversation about fifty times, and for some reason the end result is always the same: I pour the fruit smoothie down the drain and she becomes mortally offended at my rudeness and ingratitude—not to mention the waste of ingredients that "cost an arm and a leg." Seeing the Cuisinart immediately cued me to the fact that this scenario would soon transpire again.

She also brought a set of yoga tapes "for relaxation" (although how I could relax with her hovering over me asking me every minute how I feel, I don't know), some scented candles (although I'm allergic to scented candles), and a few tee shirts that she picked up for me in colors that I don't wear. My mother is always buying me clothes I don't like. Her assumption is that if I wore more pink, I would attract all those men who have as yet failed to notice me.

"Men like a feminine look," she says. "You wear too much black and brown."

"I like black and brown."

"You look better in lighter colors."

"I don't think so."

"I'm just saying that men like pastel shades."

"How do you know?"

"It's common knowledge."

You get the idea. Usually, these conversations end up at an impasse regarding what it is men like, a subject that neither of us can really be called expert in: she, having married at twenty-one the only man she ever dated, and me, despite a more checkered dating career, having failed to secure one solid marriage proposal. Neither one of us, however, was going to budge in our conviction that we understood the color preferences of the male sex. She continued to buy me pastel tops, and I continued to donate them to the thrift shop on Amsterdam Avenue (where, if you go, you're sure to find an assortment of pink and light blue garments with the tags on, since no one, even the very needy, wears pastels on the Upper West Side).

On this visit, my mother began by taking stock of my apartment. "You still have this sofa?" she asked.

"Yes," I said. "I must still have it, since you're sitting on it."

"I'm just saying . . ."

"You're just saying what?"

"I would have thought you would have replaced it by now."

"You would? Why is that?"

"It's mangy."

"How is it mangy? It looks fine to me."

"If you're satisfied with it . . ."

Normally, at this point, we would have our first fight. I would scream at her for implying that there must be something wrong with me for not seeing that my couch was mangy, and she would scream back that I didn't have to raise my voice. But this time, I didn't say anything. I let it go. With a 20 percent chance of extinction hanging over my head, the state of my sofa, whether mangy or not, didn't matter that much.

"You need more light in here," my mother continued, having failed to elicit the expected response over the sofa. "You're going to go blind if you try to read in this light."

"Mom," I said, "I have cancer. Going blind is the least of my problems."

This maneuver did not work as expected. Although it took her off the subject of the light in the room, it redirected her to the subject of my illness. You'd think that I'd be allowed to be the one most upset about having cancer, but my mother's modus operandi is always to get the most upset, even if what she's upset about pertains to me and not to her. If this is what it means to be a mother, it should appease me for probably not going to be one. It's tiring enough being miserable for myself, but to have to be miserable for someone else too, and make that person more miserable in the process—that would be a real chore.

Having been reminded of my cancer, my mother sighed loudly: "I can't believe it," she said. "You've always been so healthy and now . . . this."

"I have a good prognosis," I reminded her. "You don't have to worry."

"It's a mother's job to worry about her child," she said. "But I just don't understand it. No one in our family ever had breast cancer."

"What about dad's Aunt Chickie?"

"Who knows what she had? She never spoke to us."

"Or that cousin of yours—Dorothy?"

"How would I know? I couldn't stand her."

"But she was a blood relation."

"Stop splitting hairs. No one important had it, is what I mean."

I didn't have a chance to parse her reasoning here because she started picking things up off the floor. "I'll just straighten up a bit," she said, "so that you can concentrate on getting well."

This, I knew, was a transparent code for "How can you live in such a pigsty?" But again, I was not in the mood for a fight. I even showed her where the Dustbuster was and gave her the bottle of Fantastik. I could see that scurrying around with a garbage bag made her feel useful, and so when she held up a skirt that she had stumbled across scrunched up on the floor of my closet and said, "What is this?" I simply took it from her and said nothing, instead of getting into a battle about what "What is this?" means (my mother always pretends not to know what something is when what she's saying is that she doesn't like it). I even let her put a stained tee shirt that she found under my bed in the garbage bag when, in the past, I would have clung to it and worn it the next day to spite her.

I have to admit that as my mother's visit progressed, she became, strangely, less toxic rather than more. Was this an illusion created by the greater toxicity of my cancer and ensuing chemotherapy? Or had she perhaps been chastened by the prospect of not having me to annoy in perpetuity? Probably a little of both. I certainly gave her extra points when she stopped pushing the fruit drinks after only two or three attempts and offered to make me a milk shake. She hadn't made me a milk shake since the third grade, when she decided I was getting fat. But now that I had cancer (and weight had presumably ceased to be an issue), it was like going back in time. I could once again be the child and she the mother indulging my simple desires.

And as I thought more about it, I began to understand the whole mother-daughter problem more clearly. Mothers do just fine during the initial period of low-level maintenance: singing nursery rhymes, reading bedtime stories, making cupcakes for kindergarten birthday parties. Only as the child grows older, begins to acquire independent attributes, and comes into contact with other people does mothering grow complicated. It's no longer a question of what is best for the child in vacuo, but what is best for the child in the context of all those variables that make up life in the world that said mother has herself had a hard time with. That's when most of the maternal mistakes get made and the serious resentments build up. No doubt you will say that I am stating the obvious here. This may be true, but sometimes the obvious is worth stating.

I don't want to exaggerate my mother's turn for the better. She was still extremely annoying, and you can't erase years of psychological damage just like that. Still, you'd be surprised what a return to basics like milk shakes can do to improve a relationship. It also helped that in looking mortality in the eye, I was less prone to make a fuss over every little thing. Not only did I let her clean my apartment, I even agreed to keep one of the less egregiously pink tops she had bought me.

"Now *that* looks good," she said, when I emerged wearing it—the implication being that everything else I had ever worn before in her presence looked bad. I let it pass.

We went out to dinner and talked about doctors and treatment regimens, which, to be honest, was a pleasant departure from our usual discussion about whether I was being properly proactive in seeking a husband. To have the pressure removed on the marriage front gave us both a chance to relax and even begin to get to know each other—and I can thank my pretty good cancer for that.

CHAPTER

24

My birthday happened to fall a week after my mother's arrival. I turned thirty-five, not an auspicious age for a single woman with breast cancer, but what can you do? Time was going to pass, whether I liked it or not. However, as you can imagine, my age wasn't something that I wanted to think about too much.

I had spent the morning puttering around my apartment and napping (pretty much how I occupied myself most of the time), along with trying to forget that it was my birthday and feeling relieved that my mother had not mentioned anything. It seemed I was going to escape hearing her wax on and on about how much weight she'd gained during her pregnancy, how difficult her labor had been, and what a beautiful baby I was (which I always took to mean that I had been going downhill ever since), culminating in an elaborately wrapped gift of an expensive pink garment that I would as soon wear as I would a burka. I was so relieved not to have to endure said commentary and accompanying gift that I was more than happy to respond to her request to run out to the drugstore and pick up some Olay Regenerist that she had forgotten to pack and said she had to have right away (otherwise, presumably, like those people who left Shangri-La, she would immediately shrivel up into a dried prune).

After going to the Duane Reade and purchasing said life-saving moisturizer (along with the age-defying serum and cleanser "for mature skin" that she had also added to the list), I was strolling back to the apartment when I was accosted near the entrance by Iris and Karen. I should note that these women had become fast friends as a result of my peace-keeping effort, and were often seen together speaking earnestly about things like dangerous bath toys. On this occasion, they seemed to be milling around in front of the building and seemed very pleased but not very surprised to see me.

"Just the person we were hoping to run into," Iris said, taking hold of my arm so that I couldn't move past her. "Karen and I have been having a bit of a tiff about something and were hoping you could adjudicate." It is a characteristic of the stay-at-home mothers in this socio-economic group that they mix language from their former lives in high-powered jobs with subject matter of a profoundly trivial nature.

Karen proceeded to explain the topic at hand. Both Daniel and Matthew, it seems, were enrolled in a preschool class in the afternoon. It was a well-run program overall, and Karen and Iris had few complaints about it, outside of the fact that the blinds weren't pulled during nap time and Daniel likes a dark room for napping, and the children aren't allowed to bring their own pillows and Matthew likes to nap with his own pillow. (Another thing I've noticed about these mothers is that they suffer from a kind of informational Tourette's syndrome—a compulsion to tell you things that you have absolutely no interest in or need to know.) "Anyway," continued Karen as though she were working out a high-level mathematical equation, "almost every week one of the children in the preschool has a birthday and the mother brings in cupcakes. The cupcakes are made with refined sugar."

"Except for the ones that Carly's mother brought in," corrected Iris, a stickler for accuracy.

"That's true," said Karen. "There was one mother who made the cupcakes with whole wheat flour and honey, and though the children wouldn't eat them, they were very healthy."

Whatever I was going to be told was taking a very long time, and I was thinking that my mother's face might well turn into one of those escapees from Shangri-La if this continued. "And your question is?" I asked, trying to move things along.

"Our question is," continued Karen, "Should we start a campaign to help educate the other mothers about the dangers of refined sugar, or should we keep quiet about it and simply not allow our children to eat the cupcakes? Karen is for re-education and I'm for simply saying no." Both women looked at me expectantly.

Could it be that the act of procreation set in motion this sort of thinking? Did the brains of perfectly competent, intelligent women suddenly turn to mush—or, in this instance, cupcakes—as soon as they had babies? Or was it that spending so much time among young children produced something akin to the Stockholm syndrome—the mothers began to think like their progeny, who were, in essence, keeping them under lock and key. The earnestness with which Karen and Iris appeared to take this issue, however, made me think that perhaps I was missing something, so I gave it my best shot. I said that I thought it would not be useful to try to re-educate the other mothers, who might resent such interference. As for preventing their children from eating the cupcakes, that would also not be advisable: it would make

Daniel and Matthew feel bad and possibly exaggerate their outsider status (and Daniel and Matthew, as I saw it, needed all the friends they could get).

"What should we do, then?" Karen cast her maternal doe eyes up at me.

"To be perfectly honest, I don't think you should do anything," I said.

"Are you saying we should let them eat the cupcakes?" asked Karen, looking slightly aghast, both at the idea of refined sugar entering her child's bloodstream and because doing nothing had never occurred to her.

"Yes," I said. "Just let it go." I realized as I said it that "letting it go" might be the best prescription for mothering there was.

With this pronouncement, I felt I had done my duty and wanted to get back, since my own mother would already be worrying that I'd been hit by a car—the all-purpose catastrophe she fears whenever I'm late for anything. I therefore tried to extricate myself from Iris's grip, but she would not release me, and my heart went out for a moment to the pugnacious Daniel, who had experienced this grip on many occasions.

"But what about the addictive properties of sugar? Don't you think it's a slippery slope from sugar to dope to crack cocaine?" asked Karen.

I was trying to frame an answer to this question, but noticed that both women had stopped paying attention to me and were gesticulating over my head at someone. "OK, we can let her go now," said Karen. Iris let go of my arm and I walked into the lobby.

"Surprise!" everyone yelled.

Yes, it was a surprise party *for me*. I immediately assumed that my mother was behind it because it combined two things I don't like: my birthday and any kind of surprise, which tends either to be bad (remember Eleanor's dictum) or likely to catch me wearing an unflattering outfit. Nonetheless, when you are being feted like this, you have to rise to the occasion or everyone gets annoyed.

"Oh my God!" I therefore said on cue. "I can't believe it! How did you know?"

It turned out that the idea had actually originated with Pedro, who, for some unknown reason, had access to the birthdays of everyone in the building and who had spoken to the tenants who knew me. My mother had also been commandeered, along with Pauline, to provide the balloons and the cake, which read "Happy Birthday Suzanne from your friends on West 76th Street." After the hilarity attached to my surprise had died down, Pedro presented me with a locket inscribed with the address of the building, useful in the event that I developed Alzheimer's and forgot where I lived. Soon everyone was singing "Happy Birthday" with the cheerfulness that comes from being grateful that it is not their birthday being celebrated.

Despite my opposition to such things in principle, I was moved. All these people had made the effort to come downstairs to wish me well. There were Philip and Kurt, the playground mothers, the old Jews (even Mrs. Schwartz with her walker and Brodsky, who was staring at all the women's boobs), along with some people I'd never seen before but who nonetheless were eager to wish me happy birthday and take a piece of cake.

Stephen, the not-so-wispy math teacher, was there—or at least, happened to be passing through the lobby at the height of the festivities. He seemed distracted, but he nonetheless waited near the front desk to greet me as I negotiated the tide of well-wishers. I had continued to run into him now and then in the elevator and the mailroom, and he had continued to look less and less wispy—indeed, he had not looked wispy at all, though I had tried to think of him this way because this is how I operate, at least according to Dr. Chitturi: I find some negative, often entirely nonexistent characteristic in someone I might like so as to keep said person at arm's length and thereby deprive myself of achieving the sort of intimacy that I apparently crave but am afraid to experience.

Of course, Stephen's growing lack of wispiness was also attributable, as I noted before, to his being attached to someone else. I had seen him once in the lobby with the attractive blond, whose role in his life had been confirmed when I sighted him again conversing intensely with her in the Starbucks on Broadway. They were seated at a small table in the corner, their heads close together in the way of people who are hammering out a lifelong relationship. I always assume when I see people leaning close to each other and speaking without interruption for extended periods that they are talking about things like what kind of down payment they can afford on a house and how many children they will have. I can't think of anything else that would involve such intense concentration. For me, talking to someone at Starbucks progresses by fits and starts, with a lot of staring at the biscotti and trying to decide if I want one, and then trying to figure out what to say while I calculate how many calories I'm going to regret if I order the biscotti with or without macadamia nuts. So when I see people who don't even glance at the biscotti, I have to imagine that they have jumped to a level of intimacy that I have yet to experience.

If the Starbucks sighting wasn't enough, I had also seen Stephen hurrying out of the building with the same blond woman a few days later when I came down to check the mail. Pedro, who had become something of a confidante, told me that Stephen Danziger was now often in company with said blond—leaving in the morning and not coming back until the next day. "Let's hope she lives nearby and he doesn't have to schlep even further to get to his school in the South Bronx," noted Pedro, his speech now predictably inflected by the locutions of the old Jews. I didn't say anything—only registering the fact that I'd lost my chance. The no-longer-wispy Stephen had been snapped up.

On the occasion of my surprise birthday party, however, he lingered near the front desk, and when I finally made my way through the birthday throng to where he was waiting, I noticed that his eyes were a kind of bluish-gray, the color of my father's, and that his smile was even kinder than I had noticed before. After I greeted him, he took my hand and looked at me a moment with the sort of genuine interest that you rarely see, except from blood relatives who have been conditioned to care about you. "Happy birthday, Suzanne," he said. The use of my name, I have to say, touched me. In my experience, most people don't use names with any consideration; they throw them around like arbitrary placeholders. Only occasionally do you find someone who connects the name to the person they're talking to, which can produce a very novel and personalized effect. Stephen, it appeared, was one of those people.

"I'd like to stay, but I have an appointment and don't want to be late," he muttered, which I assumed was code for "I'm deeply involved with a caring but very sexy blond woman, and I don't want to keep her waiting." Still, he did hold my hand a fraction longer than was called for—believe me, I'm calibrated to notice these things—which, I assume, was his way of saying "I kind of like you, and if only you'd noticed me earlier—and maybe not pretended to forget my name—who knows what there might have been between us?" Fortunately, I couldn't concentrate on this missed opportunity and feel as bad about it as I might have since I was preoccupied with having cancer and because Pedro, with the help of my mother, had orchestrated the birthday party currently taking place in the lobby of my building. Thank God for distractions.

"Who's that?" said my mother, after Stephen had left and she had wended her way to my side. My mother, needless to say, has the eyes of a hawk where men of a certain age are concerned.

"I have no idea," I said.

"Yes, you do. He used your name. I heard him."

How could my mother have known he used my name when she was across the lobby? Most of the time she is partially deaf, but where she has no business hearing, her hearing is perfect.

Pauline, who had been helping my mother cut the cake, chimed in, "That's Stephen Danziger. I had him in mind for Suzanne for a while."

"Really?" said my mother. "Danziger. Maybe he's related to the kosher foods people. What does he do?"

"He teaches math in a high school in the South Bronx."

"Hmm," said my mother doubtfully. "Does he have tenure?"

"I think so."

"I suppose that's all right, then. He won't get rich teaching high school and he might get killed in the South Bronx, but if he has tenure, there's security. That's good."

I said I was relieved that she approved. Now the wedding could proceed unimpeded.

"Maybe he could transfer to a school in Manhattan," she noted. "It would be easier for you both."

"Mom, I don't even know the man. And he happens to be dating someone else anyway."

"He's not married yet, is he?" It was my mother's philosophy that anyone who hadn't walked down the aisle was fair game. "Pauline says he would be right for you. Are you saying that she doesn't know what she's talking about?"

This is a typical maneuver on my mother's part: if you don't agree with her, it means insulting some innocent bystander. In the past, such manipulation would send me into irate sputtering, but this was the kinder and gentler me. I let it go, just as I had suggested that Iris and Karen do with regard to the cupcakes. Instead, I thanked Pedro, put on my Alzheimer's necklace, and mingled with my well-wishers. It was nice to see how many people I had gotten to know who didn't actively dislike me, and I had a better time than I would have predicted, though the cake, which was made from whole wheat flour and unrefined sugar, was inedible.

CHAPTER

25

I PAUSE HERE to explain the logistics of my mother's visit. She had come to "see me through my treatment," as she put it, and nothing I could say or do would send her back to Santa Fe and her intermediate sculpture classes until she had determined that it was time to go. An obvious problem, however, was where she would stay during the months ahead.

To stay with me was out of the question. Even in my new, more enlightened state, I couldn't have stood it. I would have killed her. Besides, my apartment, as she herself had always been the first to note, is the size of a shoebox, and her demands in the way of personal amenities are exacting. She requires a great deal of bathroom space, for example, and I have only a small area near the side of the sink with barely enough room for my toothbrush. There is also no floor space where she can lay out the sweaters and hairbrushes that she washes out by hand every night. I don't have an ironing board or, for that matter, an iron, and I own only two pots.

"What if you want to make a pasta, a sauce, and a vegetable? What do you use?" she asked me.

"First, I would never make three things," I explained. "And second, everything I make is microwavable, which means I don't need a pot to begin with."

In the past, such a statement would have been the prelude to a fight—and my mother might even have run off to Williams-Sonoma and bought me a whole set of kitchenware that I would then have been obliged to donate to the thrift shop on Amsterdam Avenue for the gourmet homeless. But my condition kept her in check, and she contented herself with looking grieved and sighing loudly.

But back to the issue of her lodging. Fortunately for both of us, Eleanor has a very large apartment, with three spacious bathrooms and a well-appointed kitchen, all newly renovated with Ronnie's ill-gained lucre. Eleanor has known my mother almost as long as I have, but with the salient difference that my mother is not her mother and is therefore a lot more tolerable to her. Eleanor, in fact, kind of likes my mother, or pretends to. It was therefore agreed that she would take her in for the ensuing months. All that stood in the way was the dog.

My mother is one of those people who do not understand the concept of a dog. As she put it: "Why bother? They just eat a lot and make a mess. Then they die and make you feel guilty for not having treated them better." This, if I took a turn for the worse, could describe her feelings about me, but I didn't say anything.

Despite her initial resistance, my mother ended up warming to Wordsworth, which was not really surprising. Both my mother and Wordsworth are extremely stubborn, but given that my mother's IQ is higher, her stubbornness could prevail, which provided her the dual gratification of respecting her antagonist for being like her and reinforcing her superiority by making him bend to her will. If Wordsworth didn't want to walk, for example, she gave him the sort of look she used to give my father, put him in his crate, and let him stew. Finally, he walked. In other words, Wordsworth was no match for my mother, and very quickly he knew it and did whatever she said. In return, she proclaimed that he was the only dog she had ever known that she could tolerate. She even brushed him so that Eleanor did not have to be yelled at by the groomer on York Avenue. "He has very good hair," she said, "very soft and manageable, if you take care of it." I suspected that she thought Wordsworth's hair was better than my hair.

The little I had of it. My hair had grown sparse over the past several weeks, and it now seemed time for me to buy a wig. Eleanor and I had agreed to go to Wig-a-Little in the Village, for which Eleanor retrieved the discount coupon from the welcome packet that she had filed away in her Kate Spade accordion folder. We trekked downtown and spent a few hours trying on wigs. At one point, Eleanor tried on a black wig in a Prince Valiant style that made her look like Tommy Sadowsky in junior high school. This got us both laughing hysterically, and I think the proprietor of Wig-a-Little would have thrown us out had it not been so clear that I had cancer and therefore had to be indulged, laughter being the best medicine and all that.

After a good deal of raucous giggling, screaming, and passing of wigs back and forth, I finally settled on a straight-haired blondish wig that gave me a sleek if slightly alien look. On several occasions when I wore it, I would catch a glimpse of myself in a store window and not recognize the reflection. The person I saw struck me as quite attractive, someone I might have been envious of in the past.

My mother said the wig looked fine, though she preferred my real hair. This may have been the first time she said she liked something natural about me—an effect blunted by the fact that it was something I no longer had. Leave it to my mother to like my hair when it was gone.

So I was wearing my new wig in the elevator one day when Stephen Danziger happened to get in on the fourth floor. I hadn't seen him since he had wished me happy birthday during my surprise party in the lobby. As we rode the elevator together, I was again struck by how much better he looked than I had initially thought. It was true that his hairline was receding, which meant that he seemed fated to resort at some point to the depressing comb-over. All men—with the exception of those bushy-haired types who never lose their hair and end up making the women they're with look balding by comparison—must succumb to the comb-over for an interim period, until they finally arrive at that point where all vanity has been stripped away and they give in to being bald—a moment I could now empathize with, having achieved this state myself. But incipient baldness is not a crime, even if in my younger and greener days I might have viewed it that way—and I couldn't even say that it was a major detriment to his appearance. He was not a strikingly handsome man, so he didn't have that much to lose. Nor did he seem inclined to gussy himself up as was the case with Derek, who, I may have neglected to note, was extremely vain and had a large collection of hair- and skin-care products taking up space in his bathroom, not to mention stacks of geometrically patterned sweaters crowding the shelves of his closets. Stephen was also rather thin, even a bit on the bony side, which I prefer to a more muscular physique, which tends to grow paunchy with age. His eyes were a bit bloodshot, which could mean either a taste for drink or a tendency to read in poor light, but given his otherwise wholesome appearance (and his membership in Pauline's demanding book club), the latter seemed more likely. Once again, I was struck by the color of his eyes, the blue-grey of my father's, and by the fact that they looked extremely kind.

"Suzanne," he said as we went down in the elevator on this occasion, "nice to see you again."

I would have liked to show him that at least I remembered his name, which I had not been able to do at my party, owing to the hubbub. But perhaps as a result of my earlier memory lapse, he quickly beat me to it. "Stephen Danziger," he announced simply.

"Of course," I said. "How's your puppy?" I was pleased to at least have the chance to remember his dog.

"Oh, it wasn't my dog," said Stephen. He hesitated as though not sure whether to explain, which I assumed meant that the dog belonged to the blond woman with whom he was deeply involved, but he seemed to decide not to say anything, perhaps perceiving that this would be rubbing it in. "What about yours?" he asked with slight amusement. Whether he was recalling my difficulty with Wordsworth or my infatuation with Philip was hard to say. "Have you gotten him under control?"

I told him that the dog wasn't mine either and was back where he belonged.

"It's hard work having a dog," said Stephen pleasantly, "especially when you're used to living alone."

This struck me as a cogent remark. I wondered if the blond had asked him to move in, if only to help with the walking of said dog—I've heard of relationships built on less.

We had reached the lobby by now, and Pedro signaled to me that he had my dry cleaning, dropped off by my mother on her way to her hair appointment (in one of her typical acts of intervention, she had taken to going through my hamper and bringing my "more delicate clothes" to the dry cleaners). I was hoping to say a few more words to Stephen, but he glanced at his watch and looked rushed. He did shoot a glance at my wig. Men are notoriously clueless about hair, and I wouldn't have put it past him to say: "I like your hair"— only he didn't, which led me to believe that he may have discerned something and felt it best to keep his mouth shut.

CHAPTER

26

M<small>Y MOTHER WAS</small> now my companion when I went for my chemo treatment. Not that I had a choice in the matter. She decided to come with me, and that was that. This has been the story of my life. Did I mention that my mother was the only parent chaperone at my high-school prom? Not that I would have had a good time with Ian Horowitz, who wasn't my first choice for a prom date, but it's the principle of the thing. Having your mother at your prom is as good as signaling that this culminating moment in your high-school career is going to be spoiled right off the bat.

I assumed that she would now spoil chemo for me; that is, if such a thing is possible. But things didn't turn out as badly as I expected. Maybe the key is to get her in the vicinity of toxic chemicals—the two cancel each other out.

Granted, it took her a while to get the hang of things. At first, she didn't understand the joke when Flanagan said he was dying for a cigarette. My mother's capacity for irony, let alone black humor, is limited.

"I don't think he should smoke," she said. "He has lung cancer."

"It's a joke, Mom," I explained.

"I don't see how you can joke about something like that," she noted, looking sternly around at the group of us, including Flanagan.

"Lighten up, lady," said Flanagan. "Who's dying around here, anyway?"

This produced another round of laughter that my mother seemed to find confusing, but as Flanagan was the one with lung cancer and seemed to find it funny, she tried her best to join in.

She also was nonplussed by Mr. Dryer.

"Is he simple?" she asked me. "Why is he always standing around, doing whatever she says? I know she's sick, but still . . ."

"He loves her, Mom," I explained.

I saw her pondering this. I don't know that she had ever thought about love that way—as quiet, unprotesting service.

In the case of Ellen Pontillo, however, my mother seemed able to grasp the situation, and she forged ahead with characteristic determination. That Ellen had terminal cancer did not faze her; I don't believe that she thought anyone would have the temerity to die in her vicinity—and I'm sure that Ellen, though she would die, would not do so with my mother around. To make sure that this wouldn't happen, my mother's attention was relentless. She gave Ellen the scented candles and the relaxation tapes that I hadn't wanted, and she also bought her a pair of silk lounging pajamas, an assortment of educational games for her kids (geared to three grades above their age level), and a special pillow to ease any lower back pain that Tom Pontillo might at some future date happen to develop. Her supply of useless gifts was never-ending, and it was a credit to Ellen's good nature that she took what to me would have been annoying meddling as simple concern and helpfulness. Or perhaps, to be fair, Ellen appreciated the attention and actually liked the lounging pajamas.

My mother also got along surprisingly well with Mary Lou and Aidah, to whom she was continually giving advice about their love lives. "At least make him vacuum," she told Aidah about the deadbeat on her couch. "Either he'll leave because he won't want to do it, or you'll at least save money on a housekeeper."

She even made a special undercover visit to the hospital downtown where Desmond, Mary Lou's male nurse, worked on the trauma floor. She had, with the help of certain hospital personnel whom she had bullied into service, assumed a false identity as the aunt of one of the comatose patients there. After sitting for an hour at said patient's bedside and watching Desmond at work, she returned to report that he was everything one would want in a solicitous nurse—and also very cute and mannerly, and that Mary Lou should immediately leave the abusive nonalcoholic she was currently with in favor of this more gentlemanly and caring specimen. "You don't have much of a window, though," she counseled. "He's a nice-looking young man surrounded by women all day long. If you don't move quickly, he's going to be snapped up."

It was always my mother's view that men would be "snapped up." And she was usually right. Men with even a semblance of normality and congeniality did tend to be snapped up. As with shopping for well-priced apartments and sale shoes in the popular sizes, you had to make your decision quickly and move on it, or you'd end up empty-handed.

Here I should add that Aidah, who my mother had suggested might rouse her deadbeat male consort by getting him to vacuum, was herself no shrinking violet where advice was concerned. One day, after my mother had been rattling on to me in her usual style, making such observations as: I ought to get my underarms waxed since my razor left unsightly stubble, my skirt was too short given that I had the Davis knees, and I shouldn't wear green, especially on a chemo day, Aidah, who was connecting my IV, looked down and said, "Can't you give it a rest, woman? Your daughter don't need you to be criticizing her every minute of every day."

"Excuse me," said my mother, "was I talking to you?"

"No, madam, you were not. But I feel obliged, in all honesty, to say something. You ought to be making this girl of yours feel better, not worse. The treatments she come for are bad enough; she don't need to have you adding to them."

This, believe it or not, actually seemed to hit home. My mother put her hand to her heart. "Suzanne, did you hear what this woman said? Do I make you feel worse?"

Was this a rhetorical question? It went without saying that she made me feel worse; why else had I spent half my life trying to get away from her? But she had never asked me the question directly before, and that in itself seemed to me to represent a step in the right direction. So I tried to be diplomatic. "Mom," I said, "I know you mean well, but I don't need you to give me advice on everything I do. Especially right now, when I'm trying to keep a positive attitude."

She was actually quiet for the rest of the afternoon, a feat in itself, and from then on, her intrusions tapered off. They didn't stop, of course, but I could sometimes see her bite her lip as I left the apartment without the lipstick she'd picked up for me in a color she thought would brighten my complexion. She was definitely making progress, and I can thank my pretty good cancer for that.

CHAPTER

27

I CONTINUED IN book club through my chemotherapy, mostly because Pauline made sure to accommodate my schedule, holding meetings when I felt "up to it," as she said, and canceling when I didn't. This seemed more than my due; I wasn't used to a whole group of people rearranging their schedules on my account. But Dr. Chitturi explained that sometimes people don't mind going out of their way and that, instead of fighting such acts of goodwill, I ought to acquiesce and be happy that my friends valued my presence so much. "Maybe they genuinely like you and want to have you there."

"I doubt it," I said. "They just want to score 'nice' points."

"But there are many ways to score those points," she said in her liltingly reasonable way. "If they didn't like you, they could just bake you a cake or send you a card. They must like to have you around or they would not rearrange their busy schedules to make this happen."

I thought a bit about what she said and decided there might be something to it. I wasn't that interesting a person, but I could be funny, and given that book club discussion was often dominated by the insufferable Bathsheba, it might be that people wanted me there to cut the effect as well as to score the aforesaid nice points.

We had gotten into the habit for the last several book club sessions of meeting in Kurt and Philip's apartment. Not only were the chairs more comfortable than at Pauline's but the food was substantially better. One evening, after the group had rescheduled a few times on my behalf, we finally met to discuss that most favored of all book-group reads, *Pride and Prejudice*. Pauline said that it was about time we got to it; every other book club in the country had discussed it years ago.

I may have mentioned that I have a lot of unresolved anger toward Jane Austen, the result of having been given her complete works for my fourteenth birthday and thereby conditioned to believe, at an impressionable age, that Mr. Darcy was out there, waiting to be charmed by my sarcastic wit and to carry me off to Pemberley (or at least a mock-Tudor in Scarsdale). Jane Austen had raised my expectations, so that I was fated to be continually disappointed. I had grown up a lot in the past few months and become more grateful for the things in my life, but I still resented all those wasted years, looking for Mr. Darcy and coming up short. Finally, I would get a chance to trash Jane Austen.

For book club that night, Kurt had gone all out with the spread in an effort to "build me up" (that I needed to gain weight for the first time in my diet-obsessed life was the upside of chemotherapy). There was a shrimp remoulade, a pear and avocado salad, a terrine of duck confit, and a lovely chocolate soufflé, all laid out in the dining room with its country French with splashes of Italian contemporary décor. Kurt's culinary gifts greatly surpassed Pauline's efforts, and she had given up trying to compete in this arena, satisfying herself with picking the books and leading the discussion. For this reason, perhaps, she seemed relieved when I arrived for this month's group without my mother, who had insisted on accompanying me to the last meeting, where she hogged the floor even more than Bathsheba. The book under discussion had been *Wuthering Heights*, on which my mother had a lot to say, so that we all had to sit there while she expounded on how she would have "whipped that Heathcliff into shape." Fortunately, she could not attend book club this month, as she had numerous other obligations. These included grocery shopping for Ellen Pontillo and straightening up Flanagan's apartment in Hell's Kitchen, which she reported was even more of a pigsty than mine. She had insinuated herself into the lives of these people and was determined to stay there whether they liked it or not.

So, to get back to the *Pride and Prejudice* discussion, where she was, thankfully, not present, we were all seated on Kurt and Philip's plushly upholstered chairs when Pauline launched in on the subject of our assigned text.

"So why do you think this novel continues to be so popular?" she asked. "There are so many movie adaptations, not to mention all those novels that update the plot to the London singles scene or a Jewish retirement community in Boca Raton. Why do you think this is?"

"Because Jane Austen is timeless," said Karen, whose penchant for received opinion never failed to assert itself. Given her former success in finance, one had to wonder whether lots of people thinking like she did had caused the economic meltdown.

"Personally, I couldn't finish the novel," noted Herb. "I rented the movie."

"Which one?" asked David. "There were a lot of them listed on Netflix."

"The old one. It was the shortest," said Herb.

"If you weren't going to do the reading, you should at least have rented the BBC version with Colin Firth," said Pauline severely. "The Hollywood movie, even though it stars Laurence Olivier, is hardly faithful to the book."

"I liked it," shrugged Herb. (I liked it too—but I kept my mouth shut; there were larger issues at stake here for me than defending a 1940 movie.)

"I didn't expect the novel to be so funny," noted Roger. "Some of the characters are good social caricatures. Mr. Collins, for example, reminds me of that lobbyist we're always trying to get away from. Hirshberg. You know him, Derek. He's always sucking up to the mayor."

"Hirshberg is a pain in the ass," said Derek.

"I'm just saying that if you think about him as a character in a novel, it makes him easier to take."

"I don't know about that," said Derek, who, I can attest, has a very limited imagination.

"I couldn't get into it," said David. "All that stuff about visits and balls. Who cares?"

"Those things are part of the social network," explained Pauline. "It's the system that people used to get to know each other."

"To me, it's dated," insisted David. "The women are so focused on getting married. It's depressing."

"They're still focused on getting married," said Pauline, "and why not? It's normal to want to find a soul mate."

"I'm afraid you've missed the point," broke in Bathsheba. "Jane Austen was a feminist *avant la lettre*. Elizabeth Bennet knows what she deserves and won't settle for less."

"My view entirely," chimed in Derek. "Elizabeth is an exceptional woman. She reminds me a lot of you, Bathsheba."

"Thank you, Derek. I appreciate the comparison. You have many good qualities as well."

"I am touched to hear you say that," responded Derek.

Let me pause here and allow you to take in the full effect of this mannerly if nauseating exchange. Over the past few months, this sort of thing had become characteristic of Derek and Bathsheba, who had undergone a transformation after entering couples therapy with Dr. Chitturi, an event that had occurred at my suggestion. It may seem odd that I would give advice to these individuals, for whom I had formerly entertained an aversion, but having gained the "perspective thing" from my cancer, I had become a kinder, gentler person. You have probably noted this already. As the playground mothers might have put it, my heart of gold was shining through my protective cynicism. So at an earlier book group meeting, when Derek and Bathsheba launched into an altercation regarding the wound suffered by Jake Barnes in *The Sun Also Rises* and its metaphorical connection to their relationship (too complicated to go into here, but you can imagine), I intervened with the suggestion that they might want to consult Dr. Chitturi, whose work I could vouch for. They had responded with surprising receptivity, perhaps recognizing that someone who could help me must, in the parlance of psychotherapy, be unusually gifted.

I warned Dr. Chitturi beforehand that Derek and Bathsheba would represent a serious challenge, but she seemed unfazed. "Don't worry, Suzanne," she assured me, "compared to Indian couples, your battling friends will be a piece of cake." I should note that Dr. Chitturi is a great believer in "saving the marriage," a position she has honed with the arranged marriages that abound among her Indian peers. "It is imperative to respect each other first; from there, love will follow," she explained, "unless the differences are too great and the couple is going to kill each other. But your friends sound like they share many similar qualities and are physically nonviolent. I would not want Derek for you, Suzanne, but for this woman with the unusual name, he seems to me to be well suited."

We at book club were thus spectators to the results of this therapeutic intervention. Derek was trying to show Bathsheba the requisite respect, and Bathsheba was trying to accept his effort. It is true that their often lengthy exchanges, which had something of the mannered formality of Jane Austen's prose—or, if you will, of Dr. Chitturi's British Raj speech patterns, but with a powerful dose of the saccharine—were not as entertaining as the vituperative give-and-take of yesteryear, but it would not have reflected the kinder and gentler me to prefer to see human beings suffer, however entertaining that might have been.

It was after Derek and Bathsheba had engaged in this ritual of cloying mutual regard that I finally felt the need to speak up. "My problem with Jane Austen," I interjected slowly, "is that she misleads her more impressionable readers. She gives women unrealistic expectations. What do her heroines do except wait around for Mr. Right to come along and recognize their worth? It's an unhealthy model for young women to follow."

Everyone looked at me with surprise and a bit of alarm. Who would have dreamed that Jane Austen could be unhealthy? I could see Karen calculating whether she was more or less unhealthy than the Roman forum at night, which had killed Daisy Miller awhile back. "But she's a classic, and they teach her in all the women's studies courses," she noted apprehensively.

"Yes, and I'm against it," I declared. "As Bathsheba said, these novels teach women to have high expectations, but not to question whether their expectations are realistic or what they should do if they don't get what they think they deserve."

"It's fiction," said Roger. "Aren't you taking it too seriously?"

"It's been enshrined in our cultural canon, so it's more than mere fiction," I rejoined, my voice growing shrill. "It's like when they used to say smoking was good for you; doctors recommended it, so more people did it. Same with *Pride and Prejudice*."

"You think Jane Austen is like cigarettes?" queried Herb, who was probably thinking that he ought to go back and try the book again.

"I'm saying that it's good literature but bad for its readers—or at least for young, impressionable ones. I wouldn't have Rose read it until she's in her twenties," I noted, feeling it would be good to bring my argument closer to home— "for most women, I'd say their thirties, but Rose is exceptionally mature."

Pauline and Karen both furrowed their brows, considering the point. They were already worrying about computer games and vaccines. Did they now have to worry about Jane Austen?

"Do you think it's bad for boys too, or only for girls?" queried Karen, hoping that Matthew might escape danger by virtue of his gender.

This struck me as a good question, and I paused for a moment to consider it. If Jane Austen was bad for girls in giving them unrealistic expectations about men, it might be good for boys in giving them a standard to which to aspire. "I don't know," I finally acknowledged. "It might not have the same effect. But boys don't usually read Jane Austen."

"Well, I love Jane Austen," said Kurt, "not that I was your average boy. I had an Easy Bake oven and a Barbie collection. Besides, for me the novel wasn't unrealistic. My Mr. Darcy *did* come."

Everyone looked at Philip, who smiled modestly. "If you want Mr. Darcy, you might have to settle for his being gay," he noted.

"That may well be," said Pauline ruminatively. "Roger isn't exactly Mr. Darcy. But I like him anyway. I guess I have low expectations." Roger shrugged amiably at this.

"Derek isn't Mr. Darcy either," said Bathsheba, "but at least he's making an effort."

"Herb is more like Mr. Bingley," noted Marsha. "That was fine for Jane Bennet, so it's good enough for me."

Karen said that David was excellent with diapers and grocery shopping—and, really, when you came down to it, he probably did more than Mr. Darcy would ever do around the house.

So there it was. They had all come to terms with their version of Mr. Right—not quite Mr. Darcy (with the exception of Philip, of course), but somehow adequate to their needs. They were all in their way happy—not ecstatic, not without some serious glitches that required intensive psychotherapy—but hey, they were getting along.

It might have been the "perspective thing" provided by cancer, but I found this uplifting.

CHAPTER

28

A FEW DAYS AFTER I'd trashed Jane Austen at book club, I had a revisionist experience relating to this author, which I feel compelled to share before I proceed. It all started with a call from NateandClara, my fused-at-the-hip couple friends, who had moved to Edison, New Jersey, in order to have more room for their eventual family. As usual, they began the conversation by telling me how much they missed New York, which boiled down to their missing the bagel place on Second Avenue. I was expecting the usual segue into the travails of finishing their basement, when instead Nate said, "We have someone we want you to meet."

"Scott, my second cousin," explained Clara. "He just moved to New York City from upstate and doesn't know anyone."

This didn't seem an overwhelming recommendation, but I didn't say anything.

"He's some sort of biomedical researcher," said Nate. "He does something with the cardiovascular system."

"Or the lymphatic system," said Clara. "Something really neat like that."

"He's at Columbia—or NYU," said Nate, "working with a Nobel Prize winner in some hotshot biomedical engineering lab."

"At least that's what my mother says," said Clara, as if aware that the source might not be entirely reliable. "I haven't seen him since I was ten. He was really smart then; he may be a chess prodigy."

"And he's single."

"So we thought of you," NateandClara concluded.

I decided not to probe whether their thinking of me had anything to do with the prodigy part or only with the single part. In the past I would have interrogated them on this point at length and then spent an inordinate amount of time grappling with the pros and cons of meeting said biomedical engineer/chess prodigy. But the new me said, "Sure, why not?" with the result that a day later I had connected with NateandClara's cousin Scott by e-mail and we had agreed to meet at the coffee shop on Amsterdam Avenue. This coffee shop alternates with the Starbucks on Broadway as my designated site for first dates. I don't like to feel that I'm overexposing myself at any one locale. I probably opted for the former on this occasion because of my recent glimpse of Stephen in intimate tête-à-tête with the tall blond at Starbucks. There's nothing worse than embarking on a relationship that will probably go nowhere in full view of people who are deep into a relationship that is going somewhere.

So there I was in my wig in the coffee shop on Amsterdam when Scott ("I'll be wearing a brown jacket") came in. He was, as promised, wearing a brown jacket, which tells you something about his colorfulness, literally speaking, which, I soon learned, translated into his colorfulness, metaphorically speaking. He was also very short. Don't get me wrong; I have nothing against short. The sexiest guy I ever dated was five foot two in heavy-soled shoes but carried himself as if to say, "Yeah, I'm short, but I guarantee that I'm funnier, smarter, and better in bed than anyone else you are going to meet in your entire life." This was all in his body language, plus it happened to be true, or at least he convinced me that it was true, at which point he dumped me for a six-foot supermodel who he eventually also dumped in order to marry a Barnard French professor, who, though extremely chic, is only a few inches taller than he is.

This is all by way of explaining that short need not be a deal breaker for me. Unfortunately, in Scott's case, it was. This guy had succumbed to being short in the full existential sense of the word. He seemed to be apologizing for the fact as soon as he came in the door of the coffee shop in his brown jacket.

Once he sat down, I tried to make conversation. His work was with frogs—whether it was the cardiovascular system or the lymphatic system of frogs, I'm not sure, but frogs, he explained, were his focus, more or less day in and day out.

"That sounds interesting," I said.

"Actually, it's not," he responded. "I mean *I* find it sort of interesting, but I've been doing it for ten years and so, as you can imagine, I'm into the fine points. I mean frogs have a lot going on, but you have to study them for a while to get into them, and they're also pretty smelly, which can turn people off. I'm used to it, but I have to scrub for a long time after I leave the lab, and even then, the smell can linger."

I sniffed the air and thought I caught a whiff of frog.

This was not an auspicious beginning, but then my own job wasn't so scintillating either, so I soldiered on.

"I hear you're a chess prodigy."

"No," said Scott. "Where did you hear that? I haven't played chess since I was twelve, and I wasn't very good at it then." He said this, then looked at me with that mixture of apology and longing that certain men have perfected and that renders them completely unattractive—perhaps a Darwinian way of making sure they will not reproduce.

I tried to ask Scott about Albany, where he had spent the last ten years in graduate school, but his description boiled down to "it gets really cold in the winter and they have really awful bagels"—bagels being, apparently, a major issue in his family, since NateandClara also had, as noted, a bagel fetish. I tried movies, but he had seen very few because 1) he didn't have much money; 2) he spent most of his time in the lab; and 3) whatever free time he had he used to play Second Life, which I happen to think is one of the biggest and stupidest wastes of time there is—I mean, even if I don't have a life, I'm not about to rub my nose in it by making believe I have one by inhabiting a cartoon figure and giving said figure a house in the Hamptons.

We went on to such topics as the reliability of Metro-North ("mostly on time") and his relationship with NateandClara. "I really don't know them," said Scott. "I mean I met Nate at the wedding, but mostly I knew Clara from before." He sounded wistful, as if thinking nostalgically both of his own youth and of Clara as a singularity, before she became affixed to Nate.

"I like your hair," he said at one point.

Eventually, silence set in. On first dates, I can usually get through two biscotti before I run out of things to say. In this case, however, I hadn't even eaten half of one biscotto without macadamia nuts.

Scott seemed to sense that things weren't going well, and after staring at me with that particularly unattractive mix of apology and longing, he finally said, "I'm sorry that I don't have a more exciting life."

This should have been a call for identification, or at least sympathy, but for some reason it had the opposite effect. I felt angry at Scott for not having a more exciting life—disappointed in him for being Scott and not, say, Mr. Darcy. I was supposed to have gotten over this sort of thinking, but here was a case of relapse—and relapse that did not end with my keeping my anger and disappointment to myself. Instead of reassuring Scott that, no, not at all, his life was exciting enough and isn't exciting overrated anyway? what I said was, "I'm sure the frogs find your life exciting."

As soon as I said it, I knew it was uncalled for. I saw him blink in surprise and pain before taking refuge in self-deprecation. "I see your point," he said. Why is it that people like this (and I include myself in this generalization, since I've been there) have to spell out the insult, as if to make sure to show you that they are willing to direct it against themselves if that might help matters, which of course it never does? "I mean I guess I'm not very good company, except to frogs, which isn't saying much. I mean frogs aren't very discriminating."

I knew that at this point what he really wanted was to be out of the coffee shop and back to Second Life or the frogs or maybe the bagel shop near NYU (a vast improvement over the bagel shops in Albany, New York)—anywhere, in short, except here with me.

After he had paid—he insisted on it, especially, as he said, because he was such bad company—and hurried away on his very short legs, I felt a genuine pang. More than a pang; I felt awful. You'd think I'd shrug it off. Here I was with cancer, no prospect of a husband or child, a dead-end job, and an apartment the size of a shoebox, feeling awful about being mean to someone who hadn't deserved it.

And that brings me back to Jane Austen and the realization that I hadn't been fair to her at book club. As I was sitting there feeling awful about my treatment of Scott, I remembered that scene in *Emma*, the Jane Austen novel I've read even more times than *Pride and Prejudice*, when Emma insults Miss Bates, her sad-sack neighbor, who means well but is really the most headache-inducing bore, and Mr. Knightley, who in some ways is even more perfect than Mr. Darcy, scolds her for it and she sees that he's right. Yes, I'd been a real shit to Scott. But the point was that I *knew* I'd been a shit. Dr. Chitturi had helped me to see this and so, in a way, had my run-in with cancer, which had put my life in perspective. Now that I thought about it, it also made me see Jane Austen differently. Elizabeth got Mr. Darcy at the end of the novel; Emma got Mr. Knightley—but that wasn't really the point. Being a heroine meant being decent even if you *didn't* get Mr. Darcy or Mr. Knightley. I didn't want a life where I would be mean to people like Scott. I wanted a life where I would be my best self, even if I never married or had a child or lived in an apartment bigger than a shoebox. Even if my life ended sooner rather than later.

I called Scott that night and apologized. I told him that I had cancer and the hair he liked was actually a wig, and that, given my condition, I was prone to be thoughtless. I told him that I was sure he had a lot to offer people, not just frogs, though I was not the person best suited to appreciate him, given my cancer and other sorts of baggage that I wouldn't get into. I think he was not unmoved by my effort, and I myself felt good that I had done the decent thing, even without Mr. Knightley to point the way.

CHAPTER

29

I HAVE SAID THIS ONCE, but I will say it again: the shadow of death lurking in your vicinity can change the way you see things. In the wake of my diagnosis, my mother didn't seem as bad as she used to, but neither did certain ideas that I had once thought would be the end of the world.

What if, for example, I never did get married or have a child? Would my life then be worthless? Was I to consign myself to a future of joylessness and hopelessness for the simple reason that I had not found someone with whom to share it and procreate? It struck me that what I'd been looking for had not been another person at all, but—to be clichéd about it—something in myself that would make me feel whole and fully alive. Ironically, the cancer had done this. I saw, in the corny fashion of one of those made-for-TV movies, that I wanted to live and was grateful for my life, even if nothing particular changed in it. I had a few good friends, a nice circle of acquaintances, a well-located if very small apartment in an exciting city, and a non-taxing job that in time might be replaced by another not unlike it. I had a lot to be thankful for.

It was in the wake of such existential insight that I chucked the wig for a turban. I had initially been put off by the idea of a turban. We were no longer in the 1920s, when a turban might be part of an ensemble that included a cigarette holder and harem pants. Nowadays, a turban could mean only one thing: chemotherapy. But the wig had started to itch, and so I had donned the turban and, with it, a new and empowered philosophical outlook. I didn't care that it trumpeted my condition to the world. Let them know, I thought. I'm proud to be fighting my pretty good cancer, and if anyone wants to commiserate with me, I will accept their commiseration gracefully.

And I did have my share of well-wishers during the turban phase. Women would wander over, pat me on the shoulder, and say they'd been there—or their mother had or their sister or their best friend. I've never been a sentimental person, and groupthink irritates me, but here I was being patted and applauded for my cancer, which wasn't even, as far as I could see, going to kill me. It was a disquieting but not unpleasant experience. I felt warmly toward my well-wishers, and pleased to see that those who told me they had been through what I was going through looked, for the most part, pretty good. Sometimes, of course, I was obliged to hear more than I wanted about regimens, doctors, diets, drugs, prosthetic breasts, and breast reconstructions. But it wasn't hard to listen and smile. It was the first time that I found myself a member of a club where I didn't have to exert myself to belong: I didn't have to make lanyards or sing in the choir or do community service or chatter in Spanish around a lunch table. I didn't even have to read books. It was nice to be congratulated for doing nothing.

Inevitably—and my new club buddies might have predicted this—I abandoned the turban for the bare head. It had always annoyed me to see women strutting around bald. It seemed they were asking to be congratulated for being sick. But now that I was part of the group, I saw it differently. I knew that my chances, for all the cheeriness of my child ob-gyn and my bearded oncologist, were only statistically excellent. I could still be dead from my pretty good cancer. The point was not to advertise the fact that I might die but rather to celebrate the fact that I was alive. Whether I survived in the long term or not, it was about being here—eating, speaking, breathing—right now. That's what the baldness meant, and I embraced it.

I should note that baldness does upset some people. A bald woman is pugnacious-looking and can arouse a certain amount of fear and dread. No one wants to mess with a bald woman, and so, when I got a notice saying I had to pay a penalty because my checking account had fallen below the minimum for a day and a half, I went up to the bank manager and said, "Excuse me. I've been banking here for almost ten years, and I think that this sort of customer service is unacceptable." And he backed down and apologized, saying how much he valued me as a customer and hoped that I would give them many more years of loyal patronage—which may have been a code for "I hope you don't die of your cancer"—a sentiment I could appreciate as well.

Even my mother, who was constantly telling me to put on a little makeup (even when I was on my way for treatment), inevitably adding, "You never know who you might meet in the chemo room," seemed to be intimidated by my bald head and, after a tentative question regarding whether my turban was in the wash, said nothing more about it.

The reactions I got to my baldness were interesting to contemplate. Why were some people so rattled? Was it because I was announcing my mortality so, well, baldly, and they didn't like to have this rubbed in their faces? Was it my flagrant disregard for conventional female beauty—that I seemed no longer to care about the silken tresses that our society reveres, threatening, as a result, the very basis of societal norms and edicts?

What I discovered by spending time without hair was that you can recalibrate your ideas about beauty. I came to feel that I had a very nicely shaped head (albeit with a small indentation over my left ear from where Sonia Goldstein bashed me with her field-hockey stick in tenth grade). But the dent notwithstanding, I came to like the way I looked without hair. Some people apparently agreed, including a number of young men with piercings who asked me if I wanted to hang out and hear their bands rehearse.

To be honest, in my new, bald state, I looked better than I ever had in my life: more confident, more powerful, more authentic. And it didn't hurt that I lost a few pounds as a side effect of chemo, so my clothes fit better.

CHAPTER

30

To GIVE YOU an example of the new, more empowered me, consider my part in the Race for the Cure fiasco, an incident still talked about in certain circles. Here's how it happened.

"I've signed us all up for Race for the Cure," my mother announced one day.

This was typical of her. She was usurping my cancer and making it a team sport. I do not like team sports or, for that matter, large groups of women celebrating their breasts. Although Race for the Cure is ostensibly about raising money for cancer treatment, it has always seemed to me that the two aforesaid elements eclipse the fund-raising part. But as you may have surmised, it is very difficult to oppose my mother once she decides on a course of action. And the Race for the Cure does become more difficult to oppose when you have cancer.

My mother, I knew, was picturing all of us—me, her, Eleanor, and the now slavishly obedient Wordsworth—marching jubilantly among other women, celebrating themselves, which is more or less what she does all the time anyway.

As it turns out, Eleanor had to prepare that day for a court appearance related to the tangled state of the sociopathic Ronnie's finances, which left me without a potential ally in avoiding the event. So before I knew it, I had been fitted out in a pink Race for the Cure tee shirt and pink jogging suit, and Wordsworth had a pink breast-cancer ribbon affixed to his collar, and we were on our way, led by my mother in her pink tee shirt and jogging suit, to Central Park, where a legion of women in pink tee shirts and jogging suits had gathered.

Seeing so many women in one place, some of them bald, though outfitted in pink, was a pretty scary thing, and if I were a man, I would have run the other way. There were nonetheless many intrepid representatives of the sex present, some of them survivors of breast cancer themselves as reported on their tee shirts and obvious anyway from their eagerness to expound on this relative rarity to any of the women who would listen.

At one point, I was surprised to glimpse Stephen Danziger standing next to the blond woman with whom I had seen him conferring at Starbucks, thereby suggesting that they were now as good as married. A man willing to accompany a woman to Race for the Cure has to be serious—you simply don't place yourself in the midst of so much estrogen without having made the age-old vow "in sickness and in health"; there's no clearer way that I can see of assuring someone that the sickness part isn't just lip service. Perhaps the blond woman had had her own scrape with breast cancer, though given the luxuriance of her hair, I doubted it. Instead, I assumed she was connected to the cause via a relative or friend, or simply out of do-goodism, which might be part of her attraction to Stephen, who, as a teacher in the South Bronx, was a do-gooder in his own right. In other words, the two were well matched, and I could only wish them the best.

Circumstances had made me more tolerant of do-gooders (note that I have dropped the adjective "insufferable," which I used to automatically affix to this group). But though I could admire Stephen and his blond companion for their presence at this event, I couldn't bring myself to go over and say hello. Indeed, my concern was that they would see me and come over, and I would have to explain why I was there (not that it needed explaining, given that I was as bald as a billiard ball). Fortunately, as I was thinking about all this, the area began to grow more crowded, and Stephen and his blond companion vanished from sight. There was now a good deal of laughing and chanting, hugging, crying, chattering—and all the other stuff that happens when lots of women with something dramatic to talk about get crammed together in one place.

So there we were, gathering for the start of the race. Women with microphones were blasting out empowering messages, and young girls wearing tee shirts that read "I got my HPV vaccine, have you?" were handing out flyers. Never had cancer seemed to be so much fun, which I took to be a tribute to what good PR can do for almost anything.

A whole area was marked off for the Survivors Parade, giving them special visibility and possibly additional perks. I didn't know if I qualified as a survivor, being still in treatment and not yet having technically survived (at what precise point one qualified seemed an interesting philosophical question in itself). In any case, my mother, in an uncharacteristic lapse, had not signed me up for this special group, which allowed me to mingle freely with the rest of the pink-clad throng. It was all very upbeat and "we shall overcome"-ish, the sort of thing that in my earlier life I wouldn't have been caught dead attending—but now that being caught dead had taken on a less metaphorical aspect, here I was.

Along with the many corporate-sponsored teams, many of the women had formed groups of their own, variously designated on their tee shirts with such rousing titles as Breast Reconstruction Buddies, Chemo Comrades, and Vegetarians Against Breast Cancer. As I mentioned, I have a problem with group activity—in part, because I think it incites a lynch-mob mentality but also because it hearkens back to high-school field hockey when Sonia Goldstein bashed my skull in with her stick. But I found myself willing in this instance to put my prejudices aside. It was nice to see that all these people who had had run-ins with a deadly disease were still alive. My mother, I noted, was chatting happily with a group of women, informing them of the details of my treatment with typical usurping relish, and getting pointers on handling side effects of drugs I wasn't taking but which were nice to know about just in case. Wordsworth was also having a good time. He was leaping happily among the women, who were exclaiming how cute he was and what good hair he had. Cancer runs and wheaten terriers sort of go together, especially on the Upper West Side of Manhattan, and there were quite a number of his breed in the crowd, many with the foolish wheaten cut, which made him, by contrast, look even happier and more regular guy-ish.

My mother, who usually minds Wordsworth, had handed me his leash and gone off with her new friends to sign up for a mammogram, when a team with Cancer Warriors emblazoned across their pink-tee-shirted chests approached where Wordsworth and I were standing. They too had a dog, an over-coiffed Lhasa apso, who appeared to take an instant dislike to both Wordsworth and me. This dog had turned in our direction, bared its teeth, and was growling with malevolent relish as though we were just the sort of dog and owner that it would like to bite. Wordsworth, as was only natural, growled back. I had been here before at the Doggie Meet and Greet, where Philip had been on hand to take over. This time it was just me and Wordsworth in a sea of pink jogging suits. I was, however, a more forceful and confident me than the pre-cancer version and not so easily intimidated.

"Excuse me," I said to the woman holding the leash of the growling Lhasa apso, "can you please pull back your dog? He's threatening mine."

The woman looked at me. She happened to be as bald as I was, but that we were both bald and encountering each other at Race for the Cure did not matter, since I was impugning her dog's behavior and, by extension, herself. She, like me, seemed to have been empowered by her cancer, only her empowerment had made her nasty while mine had made me assertive—although the difference between these two states, I admit, may be a subjective one.

"Delilah happens to be female," said the dog's owner pointedly, as though I had committed an act of gender discrimination by not using "she" as my default pronoun in referring to her dog. "And *she* doesn't threaten other dogs," she added, choosing to ignore the fact that her dog was pulling at the leash and flagrantly baring its teeth. My shaved head, which should have established a bond between us, appeared to antagonize her further, as though daring her to compete about whose cancer was better or worse (it's not clear to me what, in this context, the winning position would be). Perhaps she thought I was an impostor who had shaved my head in order to crash the event. This may seem like an unlikely thought, but given my own paranoia, I never underestimate the bizarre ideas that other people are capable of entertaining.

"But she's acting very aggressively toward my dog," I said, not backing down but taking what I thought was a conciliatory tone.

"Then take your dog elsewhere," said another woman, who was part of the Cancer Warrior group accompanying the dog's owner and appeared to be from the same school of pugnacious baldness.

"I beg your pardon," I said, growing testier, "but your dog started it."

"It's true," said another woman nearby, whose hair was growing back in patches. "This dog was behaving himself. Your dog was the aggressor." I was pleased to have an ally in the fight—it was rare that someone spontaneously took my side.

Unfortunately, this championship by a stranger seemed to activate the team spirit of the group allied against me. "What does she know?" asked one of the Cancer Warriors, indicating my ally, who, sensing she may have gotten in over her head, quickly slipped away into the crowd, leaving me to face this mean and hairless group alone.

"Delilah isn't aggressive," said another Cancer Warrior, who had a pierced nose along with her bald head, thereby ratcheting up her intimidation quotient. "She only responds like this when she's provoked. Your dog provoked her."

Despite my now impressive opposition, it seemed to me that this was a test of the new me. I was not going to back down. "Wordsworth was very happy minding his own business until your dog growled at him," I said. "Wheatens are known to be nonaggressive by nature." I had no idea if this was true, but I wasn't going to be hemmed in by facts. I was going to do whatever it took to give Wordsworth the upper hand.

I should add that by now both dogs were straining at the leash to get at each other, and a circle of pink-clad bystanders had begun to form at a safe distance.

The Lhasa apso's owner handed the leash to the pierced-nose member of her team. "I wouldn't want Delilah to get hurt," she said, then, turning back to me, "You owe me an apology. I don't take shit from no one anymore."

"Neither do I," I said. My mother had materialized from the mammography sign-up area, and I handed Wordsworth's leash to her.

The other woman and I now faced off unencumbered, our bald heads shining in the morning sun. We were both breathing heavily inside our Race for the Cure pink tee shirts and jogging suits.

"Bitch," said my antagonist.

"Wordsworth happens to be male," I corrected.

"I wasn't talking about your dog."

I don't know quite how it happened but I threw the first punch. She reciprocated, at which point an avalanche of pink-suited women descended on us, pulling us apart. But not before a photographer had snapped our picture. Two women in pink jogging suits with bald heads having a fist fight at Race for the Cure makes for good copy, and that's how I happened to appear on page 6 of the *New York Post*. The caption: "Fight for the Cure."

CHAPTER

31

THE I-ACE ANNUAL CONVENTION was held in the Parsippany New Jersey Hilton over a weekend in March. Although the group is, by nomenclature, international, most of the membership, as I have noted, is from the tri-state area. Other areas of the country may have higher temperatures, but they don't produce the sort of undiluted nerdishness that devotes itself passionately to air conditioning.

There were, nonetheless, a smattering of foreigners at the convention—i.e., several Pakistanis and a contingent from South America, where the whole issue of air conditioning is bound up with mosquitoes, creating a special category in itself. Yves was possibly the only representative from the European Union. He had returned for the conference, bringing his wife, Marie-Thérèse, to whom he seemed completely unabashed about introducing me. Marie-Thérèse had the aquiline features and tightly coiled chignon proper to the cold and disdainful Frenchwoman.

I had worn my blondish wig for the occasion, and he immediately said that he liked my hair, while Marie-Thérèse, in keeping with her reputation for being cold and disdainful, ignored me. When she was out shopping that afternoon, Yves asked if I wanted to go for an aperitif, and, when I demurred, shrugged Gallicly and sidled up to one of the female air-conditioning engineers—there were very few of these but he had spotted a youngish if stoutish one—and began talking to her animatedly about his no-chill system. I could see that said youngish, stoutish air-conditioning engineer was dazzled and ready to go for an aperitif to talk more, and I wondered whether I should warn her about Marie-Thérèse, not to mention Gilles and Lorraine. I thought better of it when I saw she was wearing a wedding ring. Despite her stoutness, she had managed to have a spouse of her own, which put her one up on me. If she was going to two-time her husband in (according to her name tag) Yonkers, who was I to stand in her way?

Roy, Walt, and Dave huddled around me early in the conference. They were by nature shy, and the arrival each year of so many people, albeit people like themselves, had a disorienting effect. Gradually, however, they were acclimated and drawn into conversations about precipitate levels, evaporation systems, air-conditioning set points, and other exciting facets of the field. I was left picking at the browning cauliflower surrounding the empty container of dip in the far corner of the Parsippany Hilton Grand Hall.

During the conference sessions that followed the greeting period, I handed out some of the latest fact sheets on air-conditioning standards and chatted up the media, those wild and crazy guys covering the conference beat for publications like *Air Conditioning News* and *Heating and Air Conditioning Digest*. These guys were waiting for their big break—i.e., a job with one of the sexier trade journals like *Chemical Engineering News* or *Physics Today*.

Ironically, the air conditioning in the Parsippany Hilton was not working well, a fact that became a leitmotif of the conference. Throughout the Grand Hall, men in high-belted pants and pocket protectors were swinging sling psychrometers—devices that consisted of two thermometer-style bulbs, one to ascertain humidity, the other temperature. Readings from the devices were called out at intervals during the proceedings, which caused the assembled throng to groan and pontificate on what needed to be done to recalibrate the faulty system. The dilemma would have been an amusing conversation piece had we all not been sweating buckets. Yves, I have to say, looked especially displeased since, in this environment, his no-chill air-conditioning system held little allure. Everyone wanted nothing more than a good blast of cold air, even if it meant putting on a sweater.

At one point, Dave ran excitedly up to drag me into what he said was a groundbreaking session on "moisture management in natatoriums"—which is to say, wetness control in swimming pools, a seeming contradiction in terms. The session, upon further exploration, turned out to be about how to keep the tiles around indoor pools dry so as to reduce slippage and prevent hundreds of thousands of dollars in lawsuits each year. "This is going to make the front page of *Air Conditioning News*," rejoiced Dave. "I just know it!"

I was also commandeered to attend a session pithily titled "Reassessing the Comfort Zone." Air-conditioning standards had been set in the 1930s by a seminal comfort study. Recently, however, air-conditioning engineers from South Jersey, seeking more accurate data, had gathered 100 naked people in a room and polled their response to temperature. The result: the comfort zone had shifted by a good .3 points, a source of much excited speculation. One philosophically inclined participant suggested that it might represent a paradigm shift in what it meant to be comfortable; others insisted that the important factor was not temperature but humidity. I myself couldn't help being hung up on how the researchers had managed to get so many people to take off their clothes in the interests of air conditioning.

At the gala banquet following these sessions, the keynote speaker, a venerable air-conditioning engineer from Ho-Ho-Kus, New Jersey, presented a paper proposing that a "global warming constant" be used to calculate cooling needs over the next fifty years. This paper was controversial, and said by the conservative members of the group to reflect "Al Gore rearing his head in air conditioning." After a lively Q&A, in which a group of engineers from Delaware passed around a petition objecting to political bias in I-ACE proceedings, we settled down to our rubbery chicken française and over-cooked julienne vegetables. As we finished our crystallized ice cream parfait, the awards were given out for air-conditioning innovation and service to the industry. Yves, I suspected, had hoped to win the innovation award but, according to Walt, his system was too untested to qualify, air-conditioning engineers being disinclined to rush things. The prize was instead given to a very old engineer who had done "groundbreaking work in coolants" sixty years ago.

As we neared the end of the evening, Walt got up and told the gathering that he now wanted to present a special award to someone not actually in the field who had nonetheless served it loyally and well. That person, it turned out, was me. I assumed it was a pity award, given that Dave, Walt, and Roy had been so distressed about my cancer, but I was touched nonetheless. Everyone applauded, and Yves ran over and kissed me on the lips to the apparent indifference of his cold and disdainful wife. Even Roy showed a lot of emotion for a borderline autistic person, and the amount of hugging

I received from the air-conditioning engineers in general, many of whom were of the bulky variety, added to the aches and pains resulting from my cancer regimen. Still, it was a nice event overall, and made me realize that my job wasn't so bad. It even occurred to me that if the position with the sanitation workers finally came through I might decide not to take it. I mean how often do you find a job where you can get so much acclaim for doing practically nothing?

CHAPTER

32

Not long after the I-ACE annual meeting, I had my last day of chemo. This is traditionally a big day in Dr. Farber's office. It's like a graduation, and since you're graduating, hopefully, into a cancer-free life, there's real cause for celebration. Flanagan brought champagne, and Mr. Dryer baked a pound cake (from a recipe my mother gave him). Ellen wasn't there—she had gone into home hospice—but she called in to wish me good luck and to thank my mother for the new duvet cover.

After Aidah and Mary Lou had infused me with my last dose of chemo, they did a pole dance on the IV pole. Flanagan, even with half a voice box, made a raspy wolf whistle, and Mr. and Mrs. Dryer clapped along as though they were at a church revival. It was all very weird and also kind of touching, and I could see that my mother who, though she likes to send Hallmark cards for practically every occasion, isn't sentimental, was teary-eyed.

"I'll visit," I said, as my mother handed out gifts she had spent the week picking out, including a package of chocolate cigarettes for Flanagan and a cookbook for Mr. Dryer. She had also bought several books about raising self-esteem for Aidah and Mary Lou and a striped red-and-yellow tie for Dr. Farber to "brighten up his look."

"Those are good people," she told me after we left. "Even that Flanagan has a good heart. Not that I'd consider going out with him. He's at death's door and he's too young for me."

"Did he ask you?" I queried in wonder.

"You don't have to be so surprised about it. I've had my admirers since your father died," she said.

This was indeed a shock. My mother was getting more dates than I was, and she was sixty-five and unbelievably annoying.

But this was the new me, not inclined to be annoyed about anything. Instead, I was happy—happy for her that Flanagan had found her attractive, and happy for myself that I had ended this stage of my treatment and was going to be able to go on and lead my life, in whatever form it took.

My cancer had turned my capacity for comparative thinking into something more long-lasting. My sense of gratitude didn't evaporate; it endured. I had options, real ones, while other people I had seen pass through the chemo room didn't have any. In a few weeks, I would start radiation, to be followed by tamoxifen for five years to prevent recurrence. Tamoxifen could cause birth defects, so, as I've already noted, pregnancy during this period would be impossible. But I was OK with that. I was glad I hadn't frozen my eggs and wouldn't have to worry about defrosting them—it would have been just a new, sub-zero version of my biological clock. Even my mother had reconciled herself to my decision. She'd initially been disappointed, if only because she likes to freeze things (she still has a piece of cake from my college graduation in the back of the icebox). But she'd come around and seemed to have an inkling that they were my eggs, not hers, and I could do with them what I pleased. She'd become a more accepting person—another thing, if I may say so, that my pretty good cancer had helped to accomplish.

CHAPTER

33

A FEW DAYS AFTER I ended chemo, my mother happened to be sitting on my sofa, draped with the afghan which she had picked up at one of the overpriced discount warehouses she likes to frequent downtown, sipping one of her fruit smoothies. I may not have mentioned that, having made so many new friends and having now gotten so close to me, her only child, she had decided to move back to New York to be with us all. This was not exactly my idea of a windfall, but she had improved substantially—or perhaps I had just developed more tolerance for her. And it *is* a big city.

"You can live in New York," I told her, "as long as you live at least twenty blocks away. I can't have you on top of me or I'll suffocate." I never would have been so straightforward in the past, but this was the new, empowered me. I said it firmly, and she didn't argue. In fact, she said it was fine; she preferred further downtown anyway—Hell's Kitchen, in particular, an "up-and-coming area," as she put it, which also happened to be where Flanagan lived. Not that she had agreed to go out with him; he was at death's door. But she would help him keep his place straightened up, do his grocery shopping, and get him a new wardrobe. Other than that, he was on his own.

Anyway, there she was on my couch one day looking like the cat that swallowed the canary. It's not the sort of phrase I would usually use, but I now understand why someone coined it; that's exactly how she looked.

"I ran into a friend of yours while I was doing your laundry this morning," she finally said.

I had been wondering why I had so much clean underwear in my drawer, and now the mystery was solved. She had been doing my laundry. Again, in the past, this would have sent me into a state, but the new me wasn't going to let the fact that my mother was foraging around in my dirty underwear get me angry. Soon she would be living in Hell's Kitchen and doing Flanagan's laundry. So I let it pass and instead concentrated on the other part of her statement. What friend could she possibly have run into in the basement laundry room? I would have assumed it was one of the playground mothers, but they all had washer/dryers installed in their apartments in flagrant violation of building regulations—this was the Upper West Side, where breaking the rules was more or less expected, especially if you could be self-righteous about it. Pauline had led the washer/dryer battalion: "You can't be schlepping down to the basement every time you have to do the laundry," she had expounded to the play group one morning. "Let them haul me away to prison if they want. I have a child to keep clean."

"So who was this friend of mine you ran into?" I prompted my mother, as she intended I do.

"Stephen," my mother said, as though it was obvious.

"I have no idea who you're talking about," I lied.

"Of course you do, dear. Stephen Danziger. He was at your birthday party. He's a math teacher at one of the magnet schools in the boroughs. He's thirty-five years old, never been married but with one long-term relationship that didn't work out because the girl had cats. Dogs are fine; he likes dogs and takes care of his sister's occasionally, but he's allergic to cats—though that wasn't the real problem. She was hysterical and far too attached to her mother."

"Well, thank God that's not a problem for me," I noted. "You learned a lot about him in a wash cycle."

"Yes, I did," said my mother proudly. "By the way, how can you wear that underwear that gets into the crack of your behind? It's not sanitary."

I let this pass.

"He's a very pleasant young man," my mother continued, "though he's not related to the kosher foods people. He likes you."

"I don't know him," I said. "Besides, he has a girlfriend."

"No, he doesn't," declared my mother.

"How do you know?" I have to admit that I was interested in the answer. Stephen Danziger had for some months now loomed as emblematic of my tendency to miss what was there right in front of my nose, just like the guy in the Henry James story. I assumed that by now he and the blond woman whom he had accompanied to Race for the Cure were working side by side in various soup kitchens and, in the interim, planning their wedding, a modest affair at which all the food would be organic and gifts would be donations to their favorite charities.

"I know because I asked him," replied my mother. "Pedro told me he thought he had a girlfriend, too—a tall blond that Pedro said was a knockout—but I like to get things from the horse's mouth."

"And what did the horse's mouth tell you?" I asked with some trepidation.

"That he doesn't. The tall blond was his sister. They've been tending to their mother during her illness. She was on hospice at his sister's apartment until she died last month. You see why it's always important to ask questions."

His sister—the blond at Starbucks and Race for the Cure! It was a plot point out of a bad novel. But in life, I figured, sometimes you have to settle for a bad novel, especially if it turns up something you want. I wasn't going to let my sense of weak plotting—i.e., mistaking a sister for a girlfriend—get in the way of another chance with Stephen Danziger. My heart leapt up at my mother's words, though, of course, I didn't let her see this.

But she wasn't paying attention anyway: "He asked how you were doing, and I told him you had had breast cancer, but had successfully finished treatment and were now as good as new."

"Thank God you filled him in on that."

"Of course I did. You want him to know the worst up front, so he doesn't get scared away by too many surprises. It didn't matter, though; he seemed to know about the cancer. He saw you at the Race for the Cure. He was there with his sister after his mom passed away last month. Even before that, he said he figured you were getting chemo, since you were wearing a wig when he saw you in the elevator."

I had to acknowledge that this showed unusual perceptiveness for a man.

"I asked him if he'd like to come over after dinner tonight. For dessert. Maybe an after-dinner liqueur."

I had thought my mother had backed off in the meddling department, but obviously she had not. "I don't drink after-dinner liqueurs," I said peevishly, though I wasn't as annoyed as I sounded. I was still processing the delightful discovery that the tall blond with Stephen Danziger had been his sister. "I don't even drink aperitifs," I added as a reminder to myself.

"There's no need to be so literal about it. It was just something to tack onto an invitation."

"No one asked you to invite him."

"I told him that you found him very attractive."

"I never said that!"

"So what? It will pique his interest."

My mother, let me pause to explain, has always had a tendency to say things that mortify me. This has been going on for as long as I can remember. There was the time in sixth grade, for example, when she called out in the middle of the mall, "Is that the boy you like, Suzanne?" And the time she told my eighth-grade gym teacher to order a medium-sized tee shirt for me because she was sure my breast size would increase by the middle of the year.

In short, my mother had a long history of embarrassing me, but I have to admit that she wasn't getting to me the way she used to. I'd stared death in the face, and it had changed my perspective. One thing about being dead: you won't get to be embarrassed anymore, which makes being embarrassed look pretty good.

So there you have it. My mother had obviously said things to Stephen that I would previously have found embarrassing but which I could shrug off now that I had the enlarged perspective provided by my pretty good cancer. If anything, I felt grateful to her for having spoken to Stephen, cleared up the sister-girlfriend confusion, and invited him over for a drink.

"When," I therefore asked calmly, "is this individual, whom I presumably find so attractive, expected to drop by?"

"I told him to come around eight," she said. "But I explained that it didn't really matter, since you were always around and he shouldn't stand on ceremony."

I thanked her for making my availability so clear.

"When he comes you can serve him some of that strudel your weird friend dropped off. I took it out of the freezer so it would be ready."

I had no idea that my mother had actually frozen Roy's strudel, but I should never underestimate her determination to freeze things that "might come in handy." As I said, I wasn't really angry at my mother for much of anything, but I didn't feel it would be a good precedent to admit it. You can't let people like her entirely off the hook or you don't know where it will lead—she was already doing my laundry, for God's sake.

"I don't see why I should serve him anything," I said huffily. "*You* can serve him something if you're so hot for him."

"Unfortunately, I won't be here," she announced. "I have agility class with Wordsworth tonight."

I may have neglected to note that my mother had more or less taken over the life of that dog, as she had once taken over my life. Eleanor did not seem to mind; she had met someone in her Partners of White Collar Felons support group.

"You'll have to entertain Stephen yourself," my mother added blithely.

"I don't know him, so I don't see why I should entertain him," I said, maintaining my huffiness.

"So don't let him in," she shrugged.

"I'm not going to be rude. The point is, I didn't ask you to invite him."

"And if I waited for you to ask, you'd never meet anyone. You should be thanking me instead of making me feel guilty about inviting an eligible young man who happens to be interested in you to drop by."

"He's not interested in me. He was probably just being polite."

"Then you can get him interested in you."

"I don't want him to be interested in me," I lied.

"For God's sake, just feed him some strudel and be done with it. You don't have to make it into such a big thing."

"I'm not making it into such a big thing. But I'm certainly not going to go to any trouble."

It was the old pattern. Except that it wasn't. We were going through the motions, but our hearts weren't in it.

"I'm not going to wear my wig," I announced petulantly.

My mother opened her mouth to protest, then thought better of it and changed course. "Go right ahead," she said. "He knows you're bald anyway, and he probably likes you enough not to care."

CHAPTER

34

STEPHEN DANZIGER RANG the bell a little before eight, which told me one thing: he had the confidence to be early. He was standing with his hands in his pockets. I had looked at him more closely during those encounters in the elevator and the mailroom over the past few months and found that there was much to recommend him beyond the fact that he was less wispy than I originally thought. Now I looked at him again and found additional points in his favor. He was, for example, taller than I remembered, or perhaps he was just standing up straighter, though he was still pretty hunched. He was thin, which I had noticed before, but this added to his tallness to create an impression of unthreatening authority—two things that are pretty nice to find together. He had a fairly wide mouth, a substantial but not overly obtrusive nose, and blond hair that, as noted earlier, was thinning but neatly combed. He was wearing khaki pants and a light blue sweater that brought out the blue-grey of his eyes. Once again, I was struck by the fact that they were the color of my father's and equally kind.

"Hey," he said. "Your mother asked me to drop by for dessert."

"I know," I replied, trying to sound nonchalant. "I'm afraid all I have is half-frozen strudel. I know she said something about liqueur."

"I didn't take her literally," he said, then looked around curiously. "Isn't she here?"

"No, she stood you up."

It generally takes men a few seconds to get used to my delivery, but he laughed right away—a good sign.

"Well, I'm glad *you're* here," he said.

It wasn't the most original statement, but it would do.

"I like that you've given up the wig," he added, which earned him more points, both in broaching the unavoidable fact of my baldness directly and in implying that he didn't mind the way I looked.

"I wore a turban for a while," I explained.

"My mother went through that phase," he noted, "but she finally said to hell with it, too." He paused, then added: "Your mom probably told you that she didn't make it, but then, they caught the cancer late and she was stage four. I'm told your prognosis is good."

"I'm sorry about your mother."

"She handled it well, all things considered. The day of your party was the day she went into hospice. It was as good an ending as we could have hoped for. She died a month later."

"I saw you at the Race for the Cure," I said.

"I saw you, too. But you were busy. Good picture in the *Post*."

We both laughed.

I went into the kitchen to bring in the strudel, and he sat down on the afghan-draped sofa. The atmosphere was surprisingly relaxed. We concentrated on cutting the strudel, which was still pretty frozen, and he said he was used to eating semi-defrosted food. I told him a little bit about working for the air-conditioning engineers. He told me about teaching high-school math. Soon—I can't tell you when, exactly—I began to feel very happy.

"What?" He stopped in the middle of explaining how much the test scores in his school had gone up in the past year. I must have been staring at him.

"Nothing," I said. "Just that I don't know why I didn't notice you at book club that first time."

"I hear you went out with Derek for a while."

"I'm not sure what I was thinking."

"I have to admit that he didn't seem right for you."

"I didn't even notice you at the Doggie Meet and Greet," I added. "I mean I noticed you, but I didn't really notice."

"You were busy with the gay guy."

"You could tell?"

"Of course. It was obvious."

"Oh God," I said. "Why would you have even wanted to come over? OK, I know my mother asked you, and she can be hard to turn down, so maybe you were scared. But still . . ."

He laughed. He said he knew I was a sensitive person by the way I'd reacted when Pauline scolded me for coming late to book club the first time. And that I was funny—he could tell—and he liked funny. Also, he liked my face, which, I guess, was an original way of saying that he thought I wasn't ugly.

Then he told me how my mother had looked at his laundry and evaluated his underwear in the basement that morning. "They're polyester boxers. She told me to replace them right away with 100 percent cotton."

"She doesn't approve of my underwear either."

"I know," he said—which meant that my mother must have discussed my thongs, maybe even exhibited them for his appraisal—it was the sort of thing she would do. Yet somehow it didn't evoke the expected mortification. I felt comfortable with Stephen Danziger—or perhaps it was that my mother had examined his underwear too and found it wanting, so we were in the same boat.

We went on like this for a while in what can only be referred to as flirtatious self-deprecation. When he finished the strudel, I even offered him liqueur—I actually had some ancient crème de menthe under the sink—but he said he had to get up early the next day; it was the semifinals for the math league and he had a bunch of eleventh and twelfth graders to drive upstate for the meet. But he asked me out to dinner Friday evening. The meet would be over by then, and he hoped I could make it.

That's when I said, "I'm going to have to go on tamoxifen."

He barely paused. "That's good," he said. "It means your cancer is less aggressive and more likely to be cured." Then: "You can always adopt children, you know, if you want to have them, which maybe you don't. Not that you should totally rule out having your own. But the whole 'having your own' thing, as I see it, is overrated."

I didn't say anything. I was thinking about that character in the Henry James story, *The Beast in the Jungle*, and how he could have used a mother like mine to help him out, poor guy.

WHEN MY MOTHER called that evening, it was to announce that Wordsworth had placed second in agility but really to pump me on Stephen Danziger.

"Well?" she said, "did he drop by?"

I couldn't lie. "Yes," I said. "And he was very nice."

"Is that all you have to say?"

"What do you want me to say? That I'm madly in love with him, that I owe it all to you, and that we're getting married next week?"

"Not next week," said my mother. "I want your hair to grow back, and I want a nice temple wedding."

"Mom, I'm kidding."

"Mark my words," she said. "You're going to marry that man. Have I ever been wrong before?"

All the time, I thought.

But this time she wasn't. I *did* marry Stephen Danziger—though I purposely abstain from dates on this occasion so that everyone can be free to fix their own. That is more or less a direct quote from Jane Austen—the end of *Mansfield Park*, to be precise, a novel that happens to have something in common with my story: the heroine needed to get a life and finally got one without leaving home, which is also the case for me. This might mean that my life *is* like a Jane Austen novel, although *Mansfield Park* is considered the least Jane Austen–like of her novels and, of course, I'm not—I repeat, *not*—pretending to have anything resembling Jane Austen's insight, eloquence, or wit. I am saying this explicitly so you won't run off and write nasty things about me on the Internet accusing me of pretending to have any of these qualities.

So that's it; end of story—though I will say, since some of you like to know this sort of thing, that Stephen and I ended up being married in the Brooklyn Botanic Garden because Flanagan had an old 'Nam buddy who worked there and got us a discount, and Eleanor covered the photography as her wedding gift, and Stephen's sister, the tall blonde, who works in advertising, found us this awesome caterer who managed to make kosher food (for the Kaplan side of the family) edible, and my hair did grow back, though it was *not* more manageable than before, and after a good deal of fighting, my mother and I did find a dress that we both liked since, although I told her continually that it was *my* wedding, there was no way she wasn't going to think of it as hers too.

Stephen and I pooled our savings and bought a one-bedroom with an alcove in our building (in the event that we would want to sleep an additional [small] person). It was a nice apartment that we could probably sell for a profit if, at some point, the small person got bigger and we decided to move to the suburbs and start talking about finishing the basement.

What else? We are looking into adopting from either Romania or Haiti. I intend to send my mother over to the aforesaid locales to do some scouting. I figure that if she picked out my husband, she could probably pick out my kid. Keep her busy with the big things, and she won't mess up the small ones.

Stephen is still at the magnet school in the South Bronx, and I'm still with I-ACE, waiting for the job with the sanitation workers to come through, though when it does, I don't know if I'll take it. I've gotten more into indoor air quality lately and pretty attached to the air-conditioning engineers. I even framed the Certificate of Appreciation and hung it over the thermostat.

ACKNOWLEDGMENTS

THIS BOOK OWES a debt to the usual suspects, who read it at early stages—Rosetta Marantz Cohen, Anne Hartman, Gertrude Penziner, and Kate Penziner—and to additional early readers, Rebecca Ingalls and Laura Knoll (whose communications skills have also been of great help to me). I am grateful to my long-time agent, Felicia Eth, my publisher, Paul Dry, my superb copyeditor, Beth Hadas, and the best of oncology nurses: Susan Deeney, Katherine Martorano, and Lori Napravnik. Finally, I could not have written this or anything else without my first reader and second self, my husband Alan S. Penziner.